A ROPE FOR SCUDDER

Jake Scudder hauled Hank Lassiter from the jaws of death three times in twenty-four hours. Yet within a couple of days he had been found guilty of murder, sentenced to death and set en route to the penitentiary to be hanged. However, Scudder was given a chance for redemption — but it meant he would have to rescue the victim's niece, and discover who had set him up. Whoever it was had much to answer for . . .

CLAY MORE

A ROPE FOR SCUDDER

Complete and Unabridged

LINFORD
Leicester

First published in Great Britain in 2006 by
Robert Hale Limited
London

First Linford Edition
published 2007
by arrangement with
Robert Hale Limited
London

British Library CIP Data

More, Clay
A rope for Scudder.—Large print ed.—
Linford western library
1. Western stories
2. Large type books
I. Title
823.9′2 [F]

ISBN 978–1–84617–893–1

Published by
F. A. Thorpe (Publishing)
Anstey, Leicestershire

Set by Words & Graphics Ltd.
Anstey, Leicestershire
Printed and bound in Great Britain by
T. J. International Ltd., Padstow, Cornwall

This book is printed on acid-free paper

PROLOGUE

Judge Leroy Anderson was never at his most lenient when he had a hangover, which was more often than not these last two years, ever since his second wife of three years disappeared to distant parts with his top hand and a goodly quantity of his bank balance. Understandably, the experience had embittered him, multiplying his natural antipathy towards wrongdoers at least tenfold.

Finding himself in the relatively unique position of being both plaintiff and judge didn't bother him a jot, especially since the defendant was a no-count rapist, rustler and all out lowlife called Frank Griggs, a member of the Pintos Marauders, wanted in at least two other territories according to the sheriff. Added to these crimes Griggs had been stupid enough to get

1

himself caught by Sheriff Foster while in the act of rustling cattle from the Hanging LA ranch, the judge's own spread. Griggs's fellow rustlers had managed to escape the sheriff's clutches, which was to prove hard on Griggs.

The judge had heard the case while nursing a king-size hangover. At his side he had a jug of water laced with three fingers of rye whiskey and a pinch of sugar, his favoured hangover remedy. He was a tough old bird of sixty-three, a product of his times, a dispenser of judgements based on intuition about what was right as opposed to what had been set as precedent in past cases heard back east and recorded in dusty old legal tomes. Almost bald as a coot, he stroked his grey goatee beard and chewed reflectively on an unlit cheroot. His eyes swept the room, taking in the insolent appearance of Griggs, an unkempt, well-built jasper with a drooping moustache and lank greasy brown hair. Behind him stood Sheriff

Dan Foster and his deputy Luke Curren. The sheriff was a tall, clean-cut man with an upright posture that reflected his standing as a pillar of the Coopersville community. The deputy was a good-looking youth of twenty-one, with an honest freckled face and a shock of sandy-coloured hair that gave him an even more youthful look. In a line to the left of them, he surveyed the jurors, local businessmen and good fellows all, headed by Pat Reilly, the foreman who was standing, announcing the inevitable verdict — 'guilty on all counts'.

Judge Anderson nodded then rapped his gavel. 'Frank Griggs,' he barked, having no intention of wasting any more time on this worthless cur before him. 'You're a scoundrel who has probably never done an honest day's work in your life. Well that's about to change. You're going to do hard labour — ' He paused, deliberately dragging out his sentence, 'For two years.' He leaned forward and smiled, a thin smile that stretched the whole of his face, giving him a vulture-like appearance. 'I'm making an example of you, Griggs. The other scum in that Pintos Marauders gang will soon hear about this, and as we catch the rest I have this promise — each one is going to get the same sentence plus a little extra, for the inconvenience they've caused Coopersville.'

He nodded to Dan Foster. 'Take him away, Sheriff. He can cool his heels in the town jail until the next train comes to take him to the penitentiary.'

Griggs stood up, his hands cuffed in front of him. 'Mind if I ask a question, Judge?'

Judge Anderson worked his cheroot from one side of his mouth to the other. 'Make it quick!'

'Do you reckon you're gonna live two years?'

'Why do you ask?'

The cattle rustler's voice rose with each word. 'Because I'm gonna kill you when I get out!'

One or two members of the gallery murmured in alarm and disgust.

Failing to get a reaction from the judge, Griggs suddenly lunged forward, as if to attempt to get hold of the judge's neck. When he failed to do so he tossed his head back and darted it forward to spit a gobbet of saliva that arced through the air to land with a splatter on the judge's lapel. He was instantly rewarded by a thump with the barrel of Sheriff Dan Foster's Colt .45 across the nape of his neck. He crumpled to the floor of the crude dock, only to be hauled to his feet a moment later by the sheriff and his deputy. He stood cursing under his breath as a chorus of amazement and anger rang around the courtroom.

Judge Anderson wiped his lapel with a handkerchief and nodded approvingly at Sheriff Dan Foster and his deputy. Foster was a good, solid man, in the judge's opinion, and he sure seemed to be training his deputy in the same manner. He poured a glass from the jug

5

and downed it in two swallows. Then he struck a light and slowly lit his cheroot. 'Well Frank Griggs,' he said patiently. 'I'm afraid that in that case you're going to have to wait at least four years now. I sentence you to an additional two years for that exhibition of contempt of court.' He banged the gavel sharply on the desk.

Griggs cursed all the way out of the courtroom.

The judge pulled out his heavy gold watch, a prenuptial gift from his first wife, God rest her soul. The morning's proceedings had taken longer than he had expected, giving insufficient time to begin the inquest into the death of Wilber Sommerton, the town banker, whose body had been discovered the day before.

He reflected on how the poor bastard had locked up his bank in the afternoon, then gone home, thrown a rope over the main beam in his barn, climbed up on a stool, then launched himself into eternity. He'd died kicking, which was more than he'd done in life. His wife had run off and left him and he'd just sat back and festered. Let himself get depressed and taken the easy way out. The fool! That wouldn't have been the judge's way. No sir. He wouldn't go hanging himself.

And the mental image of the banker's body dangling from the rope in his barn presented itself to him. Damn, at the inquest he'd have to sort everything out about the bank. Probably close it down to prevent a run on it, while he waited for the bank's head office to come back to him.

He became aware of the odd nervous cough and the rustle of folk moving restlessly in their chairs. He realized that he'd been daydreaming. He raised his gavel and thumped it on the desk. 'The jury is dismissed and the court is closed until two o'clock prompt. We'll begin the inquest then.'

As the townsfolk ambled out, the judge sat back and savoured his cheroot. He was still thinking of the hanged man.

Then he wondered whether he had been too lenient with Griggs. Maybe a hanging would send out a more robust message to other scum like him. It was something he determined to consider the next time he sat down in his court with a cur before him.

1

Jake Scudder lurched along under the blistering heat of the rising sun, his precious Texas rig saddle weighing heavily on his shoulders. He felt guilty about having to shoot the hammer-headed roan, but after it stumbled in the dim early light and broke its leg, there was no way it would have survived the trek across the semi desert — to God knows where!

He grinned to himself as he trudged on, his boots filling with sand and his trousers gathering the odd tear as he stumbled through tangles of mesquite, scrub and cactus. 'Guess I might be lucky to make it myself,' he thought good-humouredly, as he removed his Stetson and wiped his brow with the back of his wrist. High overhead in the cobalt blue sky he spied a couple of circling vultures. His hand went to the

Peacemaker at his side. 'But if I don't, I reckon I'm gonna take at least one of you bastards with me. In this heat I don't think I'll even need to make a fire to roast your carcass on.' He laughed at his own joke. 'It'll just be a pity if I can't find some water to wash you down with.'

Despite his dire straits Jake had not yet lost his humour. Indeed, he felt it was just about the most important thing a man could have in this bad old world. And his present situation was anything but humorous. He had been struggling for well nigh three hours in this inhospitable desert, having consumed his last mouthful of water an hour back. His tongue was starting to stick to the roof of his mouth and he was beginning to feel slightly nauseated, a sure sign that he was dehydrating.

A large twenty-foot saguaro cactus with three curved arms, which Jake reckoned made it somewhere about a hundred years old, gave him an idea.

He hefted his saddle over the lowest arm before it curved upwards. He untied his dirty green pommel slicker and tied it between the horn and the cantle then spread it out and placed a few loose rocks on the hem to form a half decent lean-to tent.

'I sure am sorry, Lady of the Desert, and begging your pardon if you ain't a proper lady,' he said, doffing his Stetson and bowing affectedly, 'but I'm going to take a liberty with some of your spikes.' And drawing out his short bowie knife from its rear sheath, he bent and lopped off the lower thorns. 'This is just in case I move in my sleep.'

Satisfied with his work, he walked round the great cactus and reaching up as far as he was able, he cut a wedge from one of the arms. 'You may be saving my life, ma'am, and I thank you. I know you don't like bits being taken out of you, but I reckon that this is a part that you can probably manage without.'

And sucking the bitter juice for all he

11

was worth, he shimmied under his slicker tent, relieved to get some respite from the blazing sun. With his mouth considerably more comfortable and his thirst at least part salved if not exactly slaked, he duly fell asleep.

★ ★ ★

Baxter Walsh was in a fine good humour. And why not, he thought as he looked out of the window of his plush private Pullman coach as it hurtled along towards Coopersville, across boulder-strewn plains, towering red rock stacks and mesquite and cactus semi-desert, hauled by the powerful Mogul eight-wheeler locomotive that he had just added to the SWC railroad collection of engines. He was a man used to success, used to achieving his ambitions. And since his prime ambition was to be the richest man in the territory, he was already well on his way to achieving that.

'Your cognac, sir,' said Norton,

Baxter's other recently acquired status symbol, a genuine English butler.

Baxter took the glass and sipped it as he watched the white jacketed Norton, a wiry nasal-voiced fellow snip the end of a cigar for him.

'I will be playing cards at the Painted Lady Saloon in Coopersville this evening, Norton,' he said, puffing the cigar into life from the match the butler held out. 'You may take the evening off.'

'You are too kind, sir. Even more generous than my old master, the Duke of Nottingham.'

As the manservant left him, Baxter smiled. He was all too aware that the man was undoubtedly a bit of a rogue. He doubted if he had ever worked for English aristocracy as he claimed, but his servile attitude and his English accent were enough to impress the people that Baxter needed to impress in his pursuit of wealth.

He settled back in his seat and savoured the cigar as he watched the landscape outside gradually change, as they hurtled passed copses of scrub-oak and paloverde. And as he watched, so his vision focused on his own reflection in the window. He was a handsome fellow for sure, with wavy black hair and a neatly trimmed moustache. Broad-shouldered and fit, attractive to women and generally liked and envied by his fellow men. Yet despite everything, all his wealth and power, he knew that it was never quite enough. There was always going to be someone with an edge, with that bit more money than him. And curiously that was what drove him. He had to keep striving forward, pushing back the frontiers of his personal empire.

He drained his cognac then clenched the cigar between his teeth. Yes, his empire, that was right! It needed extending. And that meant that he needed to develop the railroad beyond the SWC. He needed it extending south, to Mexico and then maybe east to Texas and onwards. He blew a self-satisfied smoke ring and imagined the new logo inside it. The SWC & AM — the South West Circular and Arizona — Mexico railroad had a nice ring to it.

He thought of ringing for Norton to come and pour him another cognac, but with a laugh he reached out and poured himself a hefty shot from the decanter on the table. He raised the glass to his reflection.

'So here's to the SWC & AM Railroad, Baxter my boy.' He sipped his drink. 'We've just got to sort that old fool out first. Wherever he is.'

★ ★ ★

Hank Lassiter was in good spirits as he drove his buckboard down the long zigzag track from his Curly P spread on to the old trail that skirted the edge of the desert as it picked a meandering route through huge boulders and red rock formations on its way towards Coopersville. Dressed in his best dudes, his pipe belching rank tobacco smoke and with a whiskey bottle by his feet he was looking forward to his monthly trip into town, especially since this time he would be returning with Beth, his niece.

'Just keep up this pace, you two pieces of vulture-meat and we'll get to town sometime tomorrow night,' he jibed at the two burros pulling the buckboard. As if in answer they simultaneously shook their heads, and champed at their bits. He grinned as he uncorked his whiskey bottle and took a hefty swig.

'Guess I better go easy on the old tonsil paint tonight,' he mused to himself. 'Beth is a schoolmarm after all and probably doesn't hold with liquor.'

As the trail straightened and started to run parallel with the South West Circular railroad over on his left he flicked the reins to urge the burros to pick up their pace. But again one of the burros shook its head and snickered, which gave Hank a strange prickling feeling in the back of his neck. He turned and squinted back up the trail, spying two riders cantering along some distance behind. Instinctively he put a hand to his side, and then cursed himself for a fool for not having buckled on his old gunbelt before he left the house. His intention had been to impress Beth that he was a civilized cove when he saw her, but now he wondered if he hadn't been a tad naïve. Although he'd never personally had any run-ins with the Pintos Marauders, he was all too aware that being so close to the Pintos foothills he was in their territory.

He thought of hailing the riders and waiting for them to catch up, but immediately thought better of it. There was something about their demeanour, even at a distance, that bothered him. He flicked the reins again and the burros responded immediately, quickening their pace. A look behind showed that the duo had also responded and were moving into a gallop.

'Damn me, they mean to catch me!'

And, old teamster that he was, he gave the animals their heads. But another glance seconds later told him that a straight chase would have only one result: he'd be caught — and they'd do whatever they were after him to do. The one thing he was sure of was that they didn't seem to just want to chew the fat.

A gunshot and a whistle as a bullet tore past his left ear reinforced the fact and Hank immediately hauled on the reins urging the burros off the trail into the desert. The buckboard slewed and bucked, its wheels quickly sinking into the soft sand. But on the burros tore, steered skilfully through scrub and cacti by Old Hank.

Another shot rang out from close behind, followed by the sound of laughter.

'Those bastards are having some sport with me!' Hank said to himself through gritted teeth.

Suddenly a loop of rope dropped over his shoulders, immediately tightened and it felt as though he was yanked backwards to fly through the air before falling with a sickening thud in the sand as the buckboard went hurtling on without its driver. Badly winded, yet a tough old bird, Hank heaved himself into a sitting position, a string of invective exploding from his lips. But the cuss-words abruptly stopped when he saw himself staring at the barrel of a six-gun aimed unswervingly at his chest.

'Now that ain't the kind of language we like to hear from a hog-tied old fool,' said the man holding the gun, a swarthy black-haired fellow with a scar across one cheek.

'You need to show a little respect, old man,' barked the other man with the end of the rope in his hand. He was a youth of about twenty, Hank reckoned, but with the malicious stare of a natural-born sadist. 'That way you might live a little longer.'

'What do you want?' asked Hank, his mouth suddenly as dry as a bone.

'All that you got,' returned the gunman. 'And maybe then some.'

'You're a couple of Marauder scum, ain't you?'

The youth grinned at his scar-faced associate. 'Do you think he needs a lesson in manners, Manson?'

The gunman nodded, ratcheted back the hammer and fired. A bullet struck deep into the sand between Hank's legs and threw dirt into his face. He coughed and spluttered and bit back the words of anger that mounted in his throat, for fear that the next shot would be a fatal one.

'Like Grover says, you're kind of a nuisance, old man,' said the gunman again, ratcheting back the hammer one more time. 'I guess it's time you maybe said hello to your Maker.'

There was another explosion and Hank reflexively recoiled back, fully expecting to feel the searing pain of hot metal punching a hole in his chest. Instead he heard a gasp of pain and saw the gunman's arm fly out as his gun flew from his hand together with a stream of blood. Both Hank and the man with the rope spun round to see a tall man straightening himself up in front of a huge cactus nearby.

The rope-man dropped the lasso and went for his gun. He was still reaching for it when another shot rang out and his hat flew from his head. It was followed by the ratchet of the hammer being instantly pulled back.

'I wouldn't move a muscle if I were you — either of you!' Jake Scudder barked out. 'I kinda take offence at the sight of two cowardly curs side-bagging an oldster. Now shuck your gun, mister and then the two of you vamoose — if you still want to be breathing by the end of today.'

The hatless rope-man gingerly unbuckled his belt and let it fall to the ground.

'Now git!' Jake barked.

The two men kicked spurs into their mounts and shot off.

'We'll see you again, pilgrim!' cried

21

the wounded one over his shoulder. 'I won't forget you.'

Jake dismissed the threat with a snort. 'Save your breath, dummy, and don't look back,' he yelled. 'A bullet can travel faster than that horse of yours.'

He holstered his weapon and hurried across to Hank Lossiter who was struggling to his feet. Swiftly, Jake undid the rope and started dusting sand and dirt from Hank's best duds.

'I'm mighty grateful, stranger,' Hank said. 'Those dogs were planning to kill me. But how come you let them get away like that?'

Jake grinned, revealing strong white teeth. 'Seemed the best option at the time. The fact is I'd just fired my last two bullets!'

Hank stared in amazement at the tall rangy man with a mane of gold hair and good-humoured blue eyes, then let out a belly laugh that seemed to bend him in two. 'Well if that ain't the darnedest thing I ever heard of. That was some bluff you played there, mister. You could have got yourself killed for no reason. Put it there,' he said, thrusting his hand out. 'I'm Hank Lassiter. I've got a small spread back a-ways.'

Jake took his hand and introduced himself, 'Jake Scudder, and I've got nothing except for that saddle on the cactus over there and an empty gun at my side. I had to put my horse down early this morning.' He crossed the ground and picked up the discarded gunbelt and then collected the other gun he had shot out of the scar-faced gunman's hand.

'That was some shooting, Jake. You seem to know what you're doing with a weapon.'

Jake shrugged. 'I only fire when I have to, Hank. Guns are a necessary evil sometimes, especially when there are curs like those two running around terrorizing folk.'

Hank nodded. 'And they probably ain't the only ones. They're almost certainly members of the Pintos Marauders, a bunch of murdering, stealing swine that are holed up in the Pintos.' He pointed at his buckboard that had come to rest a couple of hundred yards off, as the burros had found some vegetation worthy of their attention. 'Let's get your saddle and then get out of here afore they come back with some of their friends.'

Ten minutes later, his thirst slaked from Hank's canteen, Jake sat back and listened while Hank did what he did best — talked. He regaled him with his life history, starting with his early life in the army, then his time as a teamster and of how he had saved a local rancher's wife and young son from a band of marauding Apaches and of how Ben Harding had repaid him by giving him a narrow strip of land wedged between the Pintos foothills and his own ranch and the south-west desert that Jake had so recently struggled across.

'It's actually pretty lush ground, thanks to its water. Good enough for the few longhorns and pigs that I stock. And it's enough to keep me alive.' He struck a light to his pipe and was soon producing plumes of smoke. 'And now every damned jasper wants to buy me out.'

'Why's that, Hank?' Jake asked, as he plucked bullets from the gunbelt he had taken from one of the assailants and inserted them in his own. 'Are you sitting on a gold mine or something?'

The oldster guffawed. 'No such luck, Jake. But just take a look around you,' he said, pointing the stem of his pipe at the range they were now passing through. 'This part of the trail is passing between a couple of ranches. It's a kind of boundary between Judge Leroy Anderson's Hanging LA ranch and the Lazy H spread owned by Zach Harding.' He puffed his pipe thoughtfully for a moment, then added: 'It was his pa, Ben Harding that gifted me my place, the Curly P. The name was my idea. It stands for the curly pig tails that give me my living.'

'So why would they want your spread, Hank?'

'Water,' the oldster returned. 'I got the sweetest little stream that bubbles down from the Pintos foothills right through my place. When we get a dry summer a lot of the water holes on these two ranches dry up. Having mine would give them security.'

He pointed into the distance beyond the judge's range where a thin plume of steam could be seen outlined against the backdrop of the Pintos mountains. 'See the train there? That's the SWC, the South West Circular Railroad. The trail runs alongside it for a lot of miles, but then the railroad swings round beyond the range and comes back this way before heading into the station at Coopersville. Baxter Walsh, the railroad boss, would like to buy my place too.'

Jake pulled out his makings and started building himself a quirly. He struck a light and blew out a stream of blue smoke. 'And why would he want to do that, Hank? Would your land help him out any?'

Hank uncorked his whiskey bottle

and proffered it to his companion. 'It wouldn't have much use for the South West Circular, but it would if he decided to blast a way to the south. He could get all the way through the Pintos and open up a new route to Mexico and who knows where else.'

Jake whistled. 'It sounds as if you really are sitting on a gold mine after all, Hank. Only thing is that you don't have to do any digging yourself.'

Hank guffawed again. 'Yeah, maybe I will be a rich man sometime soon. In fact that's part of the reason I'm headed into Coopersville today. I've got to see my banker. But more important than that, Beth my niece, is coming to stay. We're the last two of the family and I've got her future to think of. She'll be stepping off that train tomorrow and I'm going to be waiting at the station.'

The terrain continued to change and became more undulating, with large red stone stacks and boulders as the trail drew closer to the Pintos. Up ahead the railroad came in view again. Hank pointed out the large wood-framed bridge that spanned a gorge some twenty feet deep and fifty feet across.

'That's called the Horse Neck Bridge. The trail goes down into the gully, under the bridge and climbs out on the other side. It's a damned fool thing if you ask me. A wooden bridge to carry those huge SWC locomotives.'

And a few minutes later they were driving under the huge timber-framed structure before climbing out the other side of the gully.

'Looks like your burros could do with a rest soon,' Jake commented some time later.

'And that's just what they're going to get,' Hank replied, as he swung the buckboard round a corner of the trail to reveal a crude wooden hut set back from the main trail a couple of hundred yards further on. There was a crude corral with three burros standing lazily munching feed. Smoke was rising from a simple chimney.

'And maybe you and me can get a bite and a mug of coffee,' he said. And raising his hand to his mouth he yelled, 'Hello, the house.'

Almost immediately the door opened a few inches and a gun barrel protruded. Two explosive shots rang out.

'What the hell — ?' began Hank, as he found himself being suddenly propelled sidewards from the buckboard to land face down in the dirt.

2

Zach Harding leaned back in his leather armchair and blew smoke rings towards the ceiling. He savoured the cheroot and beamed in a self-satisfied way at the trappings of his ranch-house study. A bookcase full of assorted leather volumes took up an entire wall, while another was bedecked with a couple of pictures amid a number of maps of the ranch and its various sections, and maps of the Pintos territory. Some of them were yellowed with age and somewhat dog-eared, having been put up by his late father, Ben Harding, and others had been added by himself. A gun rack took up most of another wall, while the large window on the other side of his desk looked out on the range that made up the Lazy H ranch.

'You did a fine job building this up, Dad,' he said softly, his eye resting on the oil painting of Ben Harding that hung beside a similar oil painting of a beautiful corn-tressed woman, Katherine Harding, his late mother. He picked up his glass of whiskey and saluted them both. 'To the old king and queen of the range, from the new king,' he said with a grin, swallowing a hefty measure and relishing its fiery descent.

A knock on the door brought him back from his reverie and he barked, 'Come in.'

Soong Zedong, the old Chinese cook who had lived on the Lazy H the whole of Zach's life, came in and bowed in the quiet deferential manner that he had always used, despite innumerable attempts by Ben Harding to educate him in the American ways of equality. He was of almost indeterminable age, and full of homespun wisdom and philosophy from his old country, which he had left with many thousands of others to seek fortune on the American railroads. A certain skill at cooking had landed him a job with the chuck wagons and he deemed it a blessing from the gods that one day a passing rancher called Ben Harding happened to smell his cooking and offered him a job outright.

Soong Zedong placed the tray with its coffee-pot and cup on the edge of the desk. 'Coffee very good for you, sir,' he said, his face wrinkling disapprovingly at the sight of Zach's early-morning whiskey. 'It will sharpen your mind. Very strong. But not strong in bad way like whiskey.'

Zach laughed. 'Soong Zedong, you are like an old woman! But you are right about keeping my mind sharp. I have an important game tonight.'

Soong Zedong nodded enthusiastically. 'This is special coffee. I make it in the name of Fu, the god of luck. This very lucky coffee!' He winked, then: 'And I also made it in the name of Chuang-Mu, goddess of love.'

Zach smiled and shook his head. 'Get out of here you old fool.'

Soong Zedong bowed again, walking backwards towards the door. 'Chuang-Mu will perhaps look kindly on the drinker of this coffee, Mister Zach. Will help find lover. Find wife.'

Despite himself Zach found himself laughing out loud as the old family retainer closed the door after him. He took a last puff on his cheroot then stubbed it out in the large ashtray on his desk. Luck was certainly something that he could do with, he reflected. Not so much luck at the card table, but luck to help him expand his empire. He needed something to make that old fool Hank Lassiter see his way to sell him that flea-bitten hog-ranch of his.

He shrugged and, leaning over, poured himself some of the strange-smelling bitter coffee. Might as well let Soong Zedong's gods give me a little help, he mused.

And what was the old fool talking about love for? He grinned. He wasn't a bad catch, he supposed. He looked at the portraits of his parents. They were both good-lookers and he seemed to have inherited something from each of them. But he had to admit that perhaps he could do with a little help in the love direction.

He sipped the coffee again. What did he say that goddess was called? Chuang-Mu.

'OK, Chuang-Mu,' he said with a grin. 'I have a lady in mind that could make a good successor to my mother as the queen of the range.'

An image of Ruby-May Prescott flashed before his mind's eye. He'd be seeing her that evening. Maybe?

* * *

Hank Lassiter spat dirt out of his mouth and groaned at the heavy weight that seemed to be crushing his chest.

'Don't move a muscle, Hank,' Jake Scudder hissed in his ear. 'Those two curs could have made their way here before us. Good thing they left us their guns.' And as Hank turned onto his side he saw his companion drawing the Peacemaker from its holster and peer at the cabin through the spokes of one of the buckboard's wheels.

'Hold on, Jake. I think it's just old Clem getting himself spooked.' And raising his voice, he yelled, 'Clem! Clem Brookes, is that you, you old fool?'

'That you Hank?' came the reply. 'Thank God. Come on out of there.'

Looking through the spokes of the buckboard they watched as the door slowly opened and a grizzled old man with a white beard appeared, wearing an old confederate cap. In his arms he cradled an ancient-looking Henry rifle.

'Hank Lassiter, you darned fool!' he called. 'You damned near scared me to death. Who you got there with you, some damned acrobat?'

Hank rose to his feet and winced as his muscles ached. He grinned as his old friend came towards them. 'This 'acrobat' as you call him looks as if he's saved my life twice today already. Once from the Pintos Marauders and once from you!' He introduced the two men. 'Jake Scudder, I want you to meet my old friend and one time fellow teamster Clem Brookes. He's now employed by the SWC Railroad as a sort of roving linesman.'

As they shook hands Hank asked, 'I'm assuming you weren't really shooting at us. How come you're so skittish, Clem? That ain't like you.'

Clem shook his head and clucked his tongue in exasperation. 'Course I wasn't aiming at you,' he said huffily. 'Just intended to pin you down while I identified who you were. I had a call from a couple of those Marauder jaspers myself the day before yesterday.'

He fixed his friend with a twinkle in his eye and asked, 'Why don't you bring that whiskey bottle I'm betting you've got in that buckboard and come inside and swallow some coffee.' And turning, he gestured for them to follow him back into the cabin where a coffee-pot was perched on an old stove emitting the pleasing aroma of Arbuckles. He propped his old Henry against the wall and pulled out an equally ancient-looking Beaumont-Adams Dragoon revolver from his waistband and laid it on the plain deal table. 'It ain't safe out here on your own any more,' he said, as he produced tin coffee mugs and dispensed coffee from the pot, while Hank added liberal measures of whiskey to each mug. 'Those jaspers called, as bold as brass, and told me to steer clear of the railroad for a week or so.'

'What did these guys look like, Clem?' Jake asked, sipping his coffee and immediately wincing at the strength given to it by the whiskey.

Clem described them as well as he could recollect, which was quite enough for the other two to agree that they too had met up with the Pintos Marauders members. 'Manson and Grover, they called themselves,' said Hank, and then he described their encounter while Clem listened with a mixture of amazement and glee.

'It sounds as if the law needs to

smoke this Pintos Marauders gang out before too long,' said Jake, producing his makings and building a quirly.

Hank had already struck flame to his pipe and was making smoke of his own. 'The trouble is that they hole up in the Pintos and with the network of canyons and blind endings an army could get lost looking for them.'

They talked for a good half-hour then Hank drew out an old hunter watch. 'We'd best be heading for Coopersville. Mind if we swap burros as usual, Clem?'

And as they swapped the team on the buckboard, Clem asked Jake, 'What brings you to this part of the world anyhow, Jake?'

Jake grinned. 'Just seeing the world, Clem. I heard tell that this part is good for your health.'

As they climbed up and Hank took the reins, he grinned. 'If you still feel that after this day is done, then I think you can really call yourself one of them optimists.' He looked down at his friend and waved, little realizing that it would be the last time he saw him alive.

★ ★ ★

Jake guessed that it was part of Hank Lassiter's nature to barter. At the Coopersville livery he exchanged a bag of grain and a haunch of hog meat for overnight quartering for his burros and themselves.

'You don't need no hotel bed, I figure,' Hank said, as they left Jubal Jones, the liveryman, to bed down the burros, while they used the crude facilities of his bathhouse.

'Hank, earlier today I half expected to be breakfast to a couple of buzzards. I reckon I can pass a night on a straw bed.'

'Well, after we spruce up a mite we'll stash our gear in Jubal's shake-down room then I'm going to buy you a drink.'

'You're fond of tonsil paint, aren't you, Hank?' Jake said with a grin. 'And what are you going to use to pay this time? A couple of longhorn steaks?'

Hank Lassiter tossed his head back and laughed. 'You, my friend, have got a cheeky tongue in your head. Don't let this worn-out old face of mine lull you into feeling that I'm too old to give an ear a good cuff when a good cuffing is needed.'

Jake slapped him on the back. 'Hank, I reckon it was a good day that you came across me. I reckon we're going to be good friends.'

* * *

The Painted Lady Saloon was the largest and classiest drinking establishment in Coopersville. It boasted a marble-topped bar, three long mirrors in the French style, brought all the way from New Orleans, a piano with a half-decent pianist, and a troupe of scantily if tastefully clad young dancing girls that would lighten the spirits of the saddest of gambling losers. And indeed, apart from dispensing copious quantities of beer and whiskey, gambling and gaming of various kinds were the main attraction for the clientele of the Painted Lady. This was no cathouse, although the girls were considered free agents to come and go as they pleased, the only rule being that if they did entertain male friends, they did so off the Painted Lady premises. It was a rule that Ruby-May Prescott insisted upon, transgression being followed by swift dismissal.

There was only one woman permitted to entertain guests on the premises, and that was Ruby-May herself. No one had ever actually known her to entertain any male friends, but it was something that she hinted might happen, if the right man came along and she happened to be in an appropriately romantic mood. And the town was full of plenty of eligible men, which no doubt was another attraction of the saloon. Men lived in hope.

The evening rush had already started

by the time Hank Lassiter pushed open the batwing doors and ushered Jake Scudder in ahead of him. Three bartenders were bustling about dispensing beer, whiskey and coffee, while the Southern Stars dance troupe performed some frills and leggy routine on the stage to the music of a youngster with brilliantined hair in a faded and oily-shouldered black jacket. Off to the side there were half a dozen fully occupied gaming tables each illuminated by a small overhead chandelier. Three of the tables were owned and run by the house, one for faro and two for poker, the others being rented out to professional gamblers who were happy enough to allow the house a twenty-five per cent take on every pot.

'This ain't a place for the faint-hearted, Jake,' Hank explained, as they crossed the saloon, the air already thick with a haze of tobacco smoke. 'Some of these guys would rook you as soon as look at you.'

'You forget, I'm a bit of a gambling

man myself,' Jake replied with a grin. 'Only thing is, I don't have enough for a stake.'

'I'll be happy to oblige you, Jake,' said Hank, reaching inside his coat. But his hand was stayed by his new friend.

'I appreciate the offer Hank, but I have a rule never to borrow money to buy into a game. If you do that then you've got an obligation to win, and old Lady Luck never smiles favourably on you when you do that.'

Hank tossed his head back and guffawed. And in doing so he caught sight of the table on the upstairs gallery where three men and a woman were engrossed in a game of poker. Like the other gaming tables it had its own little overhead chandelier, but whereas the downstairs tables were clearly regarded as fair game for any punters so minded that they wanted to spectate, this table was clearly out of bounds. A rope across the stairs couldn't have made it clearer.

'See that game, Jake,' Hank pointed out. 'You won't find any penny ante up there. They play for big money. Every Tuesday and Saturday night Ruby-May Prescott plays with Baxter Walsh, the boss of the SWC Railroad, Judge Leroy Anderson and Zach Harding.'

'The judge is the old bald guy with the goatee beard, I reckon, and the rail boss is the dude in the suit with the moustache. So Harding is the other rancher you told me about. He must be the young straw-haired guy in the purple starched shirt and dude's neckerchief.'

'Yeah, starched shirt and bleached character,' mused Hank gruffly. 'He ain't a patch on his old pa, Ben Harding.'

Jake nodded, immediately gleaning the fact that Hank was no fan of the new owner of the Lazy H ranch. 'All of which leads me to the conclusion that the beauty in the blue dress with raven-black hair is Ruby-May Prescott,' said Jake, puffing air between tight lips. 'She sure is easy on the eyes.'

And as if she had somehow sensed

that attention was being focused upon her, Ruby-May turned her head and smiled when she saw Hank Lassiter and Jake Scudder standing at the bar peering up at her. She smiled a glorious full-lipped smile that lit up her beautiful face and revealed strong white teeth.

'Evening Hank,' she called. Her eyes seemed to stray on Jake for a few moments, then: 'Hope you've come to spend a few dollars tonight! I'll be watching you.'

'You watch me all you want, Ruby-May,' Hank returned. 'But be careful or I'll get the wrong idea and then maybe I'll come a-calling on you.'

'Hey Lassiter, maybe you'll come call on me while you're in town,' the dapper-suited Baxter Walsh called out. 'I'm still willing to make you an offer, you know that?'

Before Hank could reply, the starchy corn-haired rancher, Zach Harding had leant forward to call out his say. 'How about a little loyalty, Hank. My pa set you up in that spread of yours and I'm willing to buy you out. Maybe we should have a talk ourselves tomorrow.'

Hank grinned at Jake and raised an eyebrow conspiratorially. He picked up the beer that had appeared in front of him and clinked Jake's glass with it. Then looking up he shook his head. 'I'm sorry to disappoint you gents, but I've got business of my own tomorrow. I'm going to see Wilber Sommerton, the banker. My niece is coming in on the train and — '

The background noise of drinkers and revellers had suddenly halted and Hank found himself the only speaker in the saloon that was quiet except for the continued piano playing. A moment later even that stopped.

The silence was broken by the gruff voice of Judge Leroy Anderson. 'You mean that you hadn't heard about Sommerton?'

Hank shook his head. 'Heard what?'

'Wilber Sommerton hanged himself a couple of days ago.'

As is the way in saloons, public

interest is notoriously fickle, and after a few moments' silence chairs started shuffling, cards were dealt and drink flowed down throats. The lifeblood of the saloon began to flow again.

'Damn me if that wasn't a shock, Jake,' Hank confided, as he ordered a bottle of whiskey and a couple of glasses after they had finished their beers. 'I know that Wilber Sommerton had had some bad luck but I never figured that he'd be the type to kill himself.'

'Was he a friend of yours?' Jake asked.

Hank shrugged. 'An acquaintance more like. Everyone's friendly with their banker, but few count them as friends. But I needed to see him, talk some things over.'

A female voice interrupted them. 'You seemed shocked Hank,' Ruby-May said, suddenly appearing behind them.

Hank turned and smiled at the saloon owner. 'Why Ruby-May, have you forsaken your poker game for me?'

He shook his head and shrugged. 'Guess not, huh.' He pointed to Jake. 'Like you to meet a friend of mine, Jake Scudder. He sort of saved my life a couple of times today.'

Jake smiled down at Ruby-May. 'Hank exaggerates. It was only once really.'

Ruby-May laughed. 'If you saved him once that makes you a friend of mine forever. Maybe we'll see more of you around here. Anyway, tonight you don't have any drinks to pay for,' and so saying she reached across the bar and instructed the squat head-bartender to refuse any money from Hank or Jake.

'Will you have a drink with us, Ruby-May?' Jake asked.

Ruby-May hesitated. 'I should be getting back to the game.'

And as if to emphasize that very point, Zach Harding called down. 'This card deck is getting cold, Ruby-May. I reckon it's time for you to get even with the judge here.'

But Ruby-May was staring at Jake

Scudder's blue eyes, as if hypnotized. A smile came to her lips. 'Why not? A drink with my old friend Hank and my new friend Jake,' she murmured. Then, looking up at the participants of the upstairs card game: 'I've had enough for tonight, gentlemen. You carry on and I'll get one of the boys to bring you up some refreshments in a minute.'

Jake noticed the nodding heads and the furtive hostile glances directed at him and Hank.

Following Ruby-May through to a corner of the saloon they sat and enjoyed happy banter for a good hour. And in that time Jake learned that Ruby-May was a widow, and Ruby-May discovered that Jake was a free spirit, wanted by no one either side of the law. As time wore on Hank began to feel more and more of a gooseberry. Finally, he took his leave to go for a stroll before hitting the sack.

Someways down a shared bottle it was clear that Jake and Ruby-May had struck up a mutual admiration, their heads were getting closer and each was aware of a slight quickening of the pulse.

Suddenly the batwing doors burst open and a stiff, wiry-looking fellow in a faded suit and a derby hat rushed in. He had a pinched face and shifty eyes. He looked to right and left as if searching the saloon. 'Has anyone — ?' he began in an unmistakeable English accent.

'What's the matter, Norton?' Baxter Walsh shouted down.

'Ah, you're here sir. I was looking for the sheriff or some representative of the law. An old man is being beaten in an alley up the road.'

Jake instinctively knew who that old man was. In a moment he was on his feet and charging out the door, while the crowd in the saloon shuffled, scraped and mumbled, unsure what to do.

'Show us, Norton,' cried Baxter Walsh, descending the stairs two at a time with Zach Harding close behind him.

But Jake had been guided by his ears. In a dark alley he found two men pounding Hank Lassiter's stomach and the oldster doing his best to defend himself. Almost instinctively Jake's hand went to his side, before he remembered that he had left his gun at the livery. Wasting no more time, he pitched in, grabbing the nearest man by the hair and yanking backwards. Immediately he punched him in the neck, aware from the man's grunt that he would have a moment at least before he recovered. And in that moment he launched himself at the other assailant, parried a blow at his head and delivered a powerful straight right to his midriff.

He heard a curse and saw the flash of a blade in the moonlight and ducked as it arced towards him. He brought his foot up sharply, grinning with satisfaction as it contacted with a leg bone and brought yet another string of cuss words.

A flurry of movement to his side alerted him to another murderous blow from the one he had winded and he dodged to the right. But not enough. He felt a numbing pain run down his arm as something heavy crashed into his shoulder.

'You're a dead man!' he heard the man snarl, as if he was aiming whatever he had used to hit him for a kill. Despite the pain in his arm he lashed out backwards, feeling something crack on the back of his hand. There was a howl of pain, and a running of feet towards the entrance to the alley. By the time Baxter Walsh, Zach Harding and the man called Norton arrived, the two assailants had gone.

In Ruby-May's private upstairs rooms in the Painted Lady Saloon Ruby-May tended to Hank Lassiter's bruises. 'What is it with you, Hank?' she asked. 'Trouble seems to be following you everywhere.'

Hank grinned, and then winced as he felt a spasm of pain in his abdomen. 'Yeah, but I seem to have me a guardian angel here. That makes three times you've helped me out, Jake. I won't forget it.' He swallowed the glass of whiskey that Ruby-May had supplied him with, and then pushed himself up. 'But now I'm going to hit the sack and get myself ready to meet my little girl tomorrow.'

He waved aside Jake's offer to walk back with him. 'No way, Jake. The night is yet young, you stay and have a chin-wag with Ruby-May.'

After he had gone Ruby-May steered Jake through another door. 'That's right Jake, I'm going to take a look at that shoulder and take care of that bruised hand of yours.' She pushed him into the room, a distinctly female room with pink drapes, flowery wallpaper and thick mats. In the middle of the room was the biggest, plushest hip bath he had ever seen. 'I have a bath every night,' she explained. 'The girls have a rota for getting it ready for me.'

Her arms encircled his neck and they kissed. Then she gently pushed him back and began unbuttoning his shirt. 'You are a bit of a hero, aren't you, Jake Scudder! Now get into that bath and I'll wash your wounds. But first I'll fix a drink.'

Jake grinned and did as he was bid, sliding into the hot, soapy water, enjoying the scent of rose water. Resting back, he slid down so that his shoulders were submerged. He closed his eyes and sighed with pleasure as the hot water began to soothe his muscles.

'A drink for a hero,' came Ruby-May's voice, slightly huskier than it had been before. 'For my hero!'

Jake opened his eyes — wide. Ruby-May Prescott was standing before him, as naked as the day she was born, with a glass of wine in each hand. She laid the glasses on a small wicker table, picked up a flannel and stepped into the tub. 'There's room in this tub for two,' she cooed. 'I always knew it would come in useful.'

Jake shuffled up to make room for

her. He grinned. 'Like they say, cleanliness is next to — '

Her lips closed on his and he immediately forgot any consideration about godliness.

★ ★ ★

It must have been about four o'clock when Jake left Ruby-May's rooms at the Painted Lady, despite her entreaties for him to stay.

'I have to think of the lady's reputation,' he whispered, kissing her nose and edging his way out.

'Come see me in the morning,' she sighed. 'Promise!'

Jake's mind was in a rare state of delirium as he made his way back to the livery barn. All in all it had been one hell of a day.

He was as quiet as he could be in letting himself into Jubal Jones's shake-down room. 'It's as quiet as the grave in here,' he thought to himself, having quite expected to hear Hank snore. He grinned to himself.

He didn't hear the assailants. All he was aware of was a sudden exploding pain in his head before he pitched forward in the darkness.

3

Jake felt as if he was drowning. He felt a sudden shock as cold water hit his face like a battering ram, and then he was gasping as water filled his nose, his mouth and his throat. He threw his head forward and gagged, and tried in vain to move his limbs. Struggling to open his eyes, for his head throbbed as if it had been hit with a meat cleaver, he blinked at the early morning light and slowly became aware of three dark silhouettes looking down at him.

'So you're back in the land of the living are you, you scum!' barked one of the silhouettes. Simultaneously with this he felt a heavy pressure on his right arm and he realized that it emanated from a man's boot grinding down on him. A similar weight was pinioning his other arm.

'What the hell's going on here?' he

asked, squinting at the middle silhouette, which was becoming clearer as that of a tall man with a bucket in his hands. A star on his chest proclaimed him to be the town's lawman.

'That's just what we want to ask you, mister,' said the sheriff.

'Why are we wasting time here, Foster?' barked a vaguely familiar voice, coming, Jake realized, from the man with his boot on his right arm. 'He's a lousy murderer and we ought to just string him up.'

A chorus of approval from somewhere behind alerted Jake to the fact that a small crowd was close by, watching this drama unfold.

'There will be no lynching in this town, Zach Harding,' Sheriff Dan Foster returned forcefully. 'Help him to his feet, Luke.'

A moment later Jake found himself being hauled to his feet. He looked sideways and saw a young man with sandy-coloured hair protruding from underneath his Stetson. A deputy's badge glinted in the morning sun. 'Shall I put the handcuffs on him, Sheriff?' the deputy asked.

'You haven't told me what this is all about yet!' Jake demanded.

'Murder, mister! That's what this is about,' returned the sheriff, moving aside slightly so that Jake could see the body lying spread-eagled across the crude bed on the other side of the room. It was Hank Lassiter, his eyes staring sightlessly at the ceiling. A broken chair leg was grasped in his dangling right hand.

'Looks like he tried his darndest to fend you off,' said the deputy, as he pulled Jake's arms behind his back and began to fit his handcuffs.

Jake didn't say a word to protest his innocence. His entire attention was focused on the huge slick of blood that covered Hank's chest and half the bed. And the bowie knife that was stuck in the old man's chest.

'My God! Hank! I didn't — ' he began to say.

But he never finished as the breath was knocked out of him by a belly blow from Zach Harding. He doubled up, and found himself gasping for air again.

★ ★ ★

Todd Brodie stood proudly on the plate of the powerful SWC Mogul engine as his pride and joy, the Prairie Rose, coasted into the small Coopersville station. As usual a small crowd had gathered to meet the train, to marvel at its huge stack, the eight great wheels and the powerful boiler. With its series of coaches snaking behind it, Todd fancied that it was as near to a dragon as anyone could ever see outside of a storybook. And as the driver, accompanied by Chuck Jenson his fireman, he imagined that he had just about the best job in the world that a man could have.

'OK, Chuck, we've just about got time for a coffee before we need to tank her up before we get off again.'

'You mean I get to stop swallowing coal dust and smoke while you have yourself a coffee with the station master, and Willie Deever the guard. Drivers and guards have the life of swells as compared to a lowdown fireman like me.'

Todd cuffed his friend playfully on the ear. They were both in their mid-twenties and had been friends for the better part of ten years. They enjoyed a cut-and-thrust banter. 'Go on, you son of a dog. You love stoking the Prairie Rose just as much as I love driving her around this desert. You're just sore because I'm going to make you come and drink coffee with me and Willie instead of letting you slope off to swill beer at the Painted Lady Saloon.'

Todd pulled on the steam whistle, as was his custom once the train had ground to a final halt. A few moments later the carriage doors opened and passengers started flooding out to meet friends and relatives in the waiting crowd.

At the other end of the train Willie Deever stepped down from the caboose and immediately drew himself to attention as he surveyed the throng. He was a man of sixty, a veteran of the railroad, clean shaven, straight-backed and a veritable bastion of efficiency in his spotless uniform and guard's cap. He waved to Todd and began making his way along the platform. Half-way along he stopped and opened the door of a Pullman carriage and helped a young lady down.

Most of the crowd had already dispersed, but a few urchins and loafers remained. The older ones cast admiring looks in the direction of the smartly dressed young woman. She wore a light blue toque and a grey travelling suit. Willie whistled to the nearest group of urchins.

'The lady's bags need tending to,' he announced. Then as the urchins descended on her trunk and two carpet bags, he asked, 'No one to meet you, Miss Lassiter?'

'I was expecting my uncle, Hank Lassiter,' she replied. 'I'm sure he won't be long.'

'Well, we were right on time as usual,' said Willie. 'Why don't you join the driver and myself for a coffee in the station master's office. I'm sure he won't be long in coming.'

A gangly lad had Beth Lassiter's carpet bag in his hand. He tugged Willie's sleeve. 'Did the lady say she was expecting Hank Lassiter?'

Beth Lassiter nodded. 'That's right, he's my uncle. Why, what's the matter?' Her face began to register concern.

'Hank Lassiter won't be coming,' said the boy, uncomfortably. He wiped a grimy hand across his lips that had suddenly gone dry. 'He . . . he's dead! Murdered.'

Beth Lassiter dropped her drawstring purse and visibly staggered. Willie reached out to steady her, but Todd Brodie reached her first. He caught her in his arms and swept her up, crossed the platform and eased her on to a seat.

'What goes on?' came the wheezy voice of Vernon Crabbs, the station master, as he emerged from his office in time to see Beth Lassiter's near faint.

'What's this about Hank Lassiter having been murdered, Vernon?' Willie asked, while Todd fanned Beth's face with his driver's cap.

The crusty station master frowned. 'The town's in shock about it. But they've got the murdering swine by all accounts. He seems to have Green-Rivered Hank while he slept at Jubal Jones's livery. The sheriff's got him locked up in the jail.'

Beth Lassiter suddenly rose to her feet, her face as pale as alabaster. 'Where is this jail?' she demanded.

'Ma'am, I reckon you ought to rest for a moment,' Todd protested.

'Would someone show me to the jail,' she said, her beautiful jaw firm. 'I want to look in the eye of the man who murdered my uncle. Then — I'll decide what I want to do!'

At that point Judge Leroy Anderson

pushed his way through the throng that had collected outside the station master's office. He smoothed his goatee beard with the back of his hand and tapped Vernon Crabbs, the station master, on the shoulder.

'What's the fracas about, Crabbs?' he barked.

Somewhat flustered, Vernon Crabbs introduced Beth Lassiter. 'We were just arranging for someone to take her to the jail to see the sheriff. What do you think, Judge?'

Judge Anderson scowled at him. 'I think that one look at this young lady should tell you that she needs a strong cup of coffee.' He pulled out his hip flask and gestured for the station master to usher Beth Lassiter into his office. 'A drop of good rye will also help.' He tapped his stick on the floor. 'Then I'll take you myself, Miss Lassiter. I was on my way when the train arrived.'

★ ★ ★

Jake's head was throbbing fit to burst and all he wanted was to lie peacefully on the crude wooden cot in his cell, let the headache subside and try to work out what had happened. He certainly didn't appreciate the non-stop jibing from the joker in the other cell.

'Yessir, it'll be the rope for you,' sneered Frank Griggs, who was lying with his hands interlocked behind his head on his cot in the adjoining cell. 'That damned Judge Anderson sentenced me to four years hard labour for just minding a few stray cows.'

Luke Curren, the young deputy sheriff appeared in the hall leading from the office with a tray and two mugs of coffee. 'Why don't you give your jaw a rest, Griggs? And just stop badgering the prisoner.' He bent and shoved a coffee mug under each cell door. 'He hasn't been tried yet, so we don't know if he'll get any kind of sentence.'

Jake swung his legs over the side of the cot and reached for his coffee. 'I appreciate that, Deputy.' He sipped his coffee. 'I didn't do it, you know.'

Frank Griggs immediately convulsed with laughter. 'Damn! How many folk have sat in that cell and said the same thing! Course you did it, pilgrim. And Judge Anderson will see that you swing for it. You mark my words.'

Jake turned his steely blue eyes on Frank Griggs and scowled. 'Mister, I don't know you from Adam, but you're in real danger of — '

There was a commotion from the office and Deputy Curren took a couple of steps towards the door, only for it to be thrown open to reveal Ruby-May Prescott. Her face was flushed and her eyes were open wide in alarm.

'Jake! I'm going to get you out of here. I've told Dan Foster, the sheriff, that you were with me last night.'

The sheriff appeared at her shoulder. A tall competent looking lawman with an open honest face, he shook his head. 'The prisoner is staying right where he is, Ruby-May. I accept that he may have been with you last night but — '

'I said he was with me all night,' she repeated, turning to face Jake and raising her eyebrows as a signal for him to agree with her and accept the alibi she offered him.

'I appreciate that, Ruby-May,' Jake said with a winsome smile, 'but an honest man has no fear from the process of law, I reckon. I left about four o'clock, Sheriff.'

'And that was just what I was about to say,' said Sheriff Foster. 'Skeeter Dutton, the bar-sweeper at the Broken Spur Saloon along the street says that he saw the prisoner leave your saloon about then and head down to the livery.'

Ruby-May stamped her foot and then reached a hand through the cell door to touch Jake's shoulder. 'I'll do all that I can, Jake,' she said, with tears forming in the corners of her eyes.

As she left, Griggs called after her, 'The best you can do for him is to start praying, honey.'

Sheriff Foster was still remonstrating

with him when there came the sound of a cane rapping on the desk in the office. A moment later Judge Leroy Anderson's gravelly voice called out sarcastically, 'This office of yours seems under-attended, Sheriff Foster, if I might say so.'

Dan Foster exchanged an amused look with his deputy and strode towards the office door. 'What can I do for you, Judge?'

'Just let me and this young lady get through,' replied the judge, ushering Beth Lassiter ahead of him. 'We want to take a look at the man accused of murdering her uncle, Hank Lassiter.'

Jake was instantly on his feet, hands gripping the bars of the cell door so tightly that his knuckles went white. He was beginning to feel an unaccustomed emotion — anger. Real mean anger. 'I didn't kill anyone!' he exclaimed. 'And I certainly didn't kill Hank Lassiter. God dammit, I saved him three times yesterday. We were friends.'

The judge sneered disdainfully. 'So

you say. But what I want to — '

He was interrupted by Beth Lassiter. With one swift move she had darted a hand between the bars and slapped Jake across the face with a free glove. 'You monster! My Uncle Hank would never hurt a fly, and I heard what you did to him.'

Deputy Curren moved between Beth Lassiter and the cell door. 'That wasn't necessary, ma'am,' he said in a gently reproving voice. 'The prisoner has not even had a trial, let alone been found guilty.'

The judge rapped his cane on the floor. 'Well, he'll have a trial tomorrow! Hank Lassiter was a good friend of mine and we'll see that he gets justice.'

Frank Griggs laughed. 'See what I mean, pilgrim? I said that praying was your best bet now.'

★ ★ ★

As trials in the south-west went it was a slick affair. The evidence was presented by Sheriff Foster, the witnesses were questioned by the judge, and then Jake was allowed to put forward his own defence. It was all pretty damning. The only thing in his favour was Ruby-May's testimony that she had spent a goodly part of the night with him, and that she was able to tell the jury what Hank Lassiter had himself told her about having been saved twice by Jake before they even arrived at the saloon.

'And those of you who were in the saloon last night saw how he went out and helped Hank when those two ruffians were beating him up.'

'Those ruffians, who have conveniently disappeared now,' Zach Harding barked out. Then jumping to his feet he waved his hand angrily. 'Come on now, judge. The whole town knows that the jasper sitting there did it, what are we wasting time for?' He looked pityingly at Ruby-May. 'And somehow he's bewitched our lady saloon-keeper.'

'How dare you!' Ruby-May shot back.

Judge Leroy Anderson was chewing

on an unlit cheroot. His cold, reptile-like eyes focused on the young rancher and he rapped his gavel on the desk. 'I run this court, Zach Harding. And I run a fair court. We'll hear all that we need to hear and that doesn't include outbursts like that. Now sit down!' He nodded at Ruby-May. 'And the court thanks Ruby-May Prescott for her testimony, which has all been taken into account.'

Zach Harding glowered back at the judge for a moment, his jaw muscles working as if to form a retort. But Baxter Walsh, sitting beside him, tugged his sleeve and shook his head. Moodily, Harding resumed his seat.

Beth Lassiter put up her hand and a chorus of murmurings and mumblings swept round the courthouse. Once again the judge rapped his gavel, and the room went silent again. 'You want to say something, Miss Lassiter? Go ahead please.'

She stood, a pretty, smartly dressed young woman. Everyone in the court felt sympathy for her. She cleared her throat and spoke with dignity. 'I just want to say that I want justice for my uncle.' She darted a look at Jake Scudder, sitting in the dock, his hands cuffed in front of him. She blushed. 'But I don't want revenge.'

Once she had sat down the judge began his summing up. It was done curtly but competently. He sent them out to consider a verdict, and while they did so he struck a light to his cheroot and sipped his glass of water laced with rye.

The jury completed their deliberations in less than ten minutes. They had reached a unanimous verdict — guilty.

Judge Anderson recalled the last trial he had held in the courthouse, just a couple of days previously, and about the mental note he had made about being over-lenient. He made no such mistake this time; he sentenced Jake Scudder to death by hanging. Sentence to be carried out in the state penitentiary two days hence.

4

Chuck Jenson had fired up the Prairie Rose and was standing on the plate next to Todd Brodie, his driver, as they waited at the Coopersville station for everyone to board. It was a shorter train than usual, with just a Pullman and a caboose. A special that Baxter Walsh had arranged outside the usual scheduled trips.

Chuck prodded Todd in the ribs and pointed to the trio of Beth Lassiter, Baxter Walsh and, a pace behind them, the English butler, Norton. 'That little girl has had a heck of a time in Coopersville, hasn't she? Arrived one day to find her uncle has been murdered. Then the next day she sees his murderer sentenced to be hung, then that afternoon she buries her old man.'

Todd was leaning on the side, his

chin cupped in his hands. He nodded absently. 'Uh huh, she sure is pretty.' Then realizing that he was verbalizing his own thoughts, he shoved his friend playfully, before the expectant jibe came. 'And now she's heading back east on the Prairie Rose.'

On the station, Beth Lassiter smiled gratefully at Baxter Walsh. 'You have been so kind to me, Mr Walsh. I don't think that I could face staying in Coopersville a moment longer than I need to. Not at a time like this. I just need to get back home, to get used to all this tragedy.'

Baxter Walsh nodded understandingly. 'Of course. And I appreciate that your — inheritance — your uncle's ranch might prove to be a millstone around your neck.' He put a comforting hand on her wrist. 'Now isn't a good time to talk about it, but I am sure that I can help you. I have to stay in Coopersville for a few days, but if I may call on you when you get back east, then perhaps we could talk — '

'Talk business?' Beth queried. 'That's strange, Mr Walsh. Before I packed up this morning I had a visit from Mr Zach Harding. He owns the ranch neighbouring my uncle's, you know. He said pretty much the same thing to me that you have just said.'

Baxter Walsh raised an eyebrow. 'Zach talked to you, did he?' Then he grinned. 'Which just goes to show that we south-westerners are always willing to help out a lady.' He gestured to the large clock hanging outside the station master's office. 'But let's get you on board the Prairie Rose.' He turned and gestured over his shoulder to his butler.

'Norton here will travel with you in my private Pullman coach. Anything you need, he'll see to it.'

Norton doffed his derby hat and when he spoke it was with a curious nasal tone. 'Absolutely, miss. I'll be in the coach pantry just through the door. If you need anything, just ring and I will be there.'

Baxter held out his arm to steady her

as she mounted the Pullman steps. 'Norton used to be the butler for the Duke of Nottingham in England,' he volunteered.

Beth nodded and turned to look along the length of the train, where she saw Todd and Chuck watching her. Instantly Todd straightened up, flustered and raised his hand in a self-conscious wave. And for her part, Beth also coloured and waved back, before being ushered inside by Norton.

Back on the plate of the Prairie Rose, Chuck Jenson grinned at his friend. 'Well if that doesn't beat everything! I do believe there was some kind of affection in that look she just cast you. Maybe the girl needs her eyes testing!' He ducked as the big driver aimed a playful swipe at the back of his head. 'Say Todd, do you figure — '

But Todd's attention had suddenly been distracted. He was watching Sheriff Dan Foster and his deputy, Luke Curren escort the two handcuffed prisoners in the direction of the caboose. A crowd of loafers began cursing and jeering at them, drawing curt remonstrances from both the sheriff and the deputy.

Todd was looking at the scene through narrowed, puzzled eyes. 'It doesn't figure, Chuck,' he mused. 'That Scudder guy just didn't seem like a murderer to me.'

It was a sentiment that Willie Dreever the guard was also feeling as the sheriff ushered the prisoners into the small cell at the end of the caboose. Once the two men were in, the sheriff instructed Luke to unfasten their handcuffs.

'You two men are not to give Luke here any trouble, do you understand?' he said, as he locked the cell door and handed the key to Luke. 'Or Willie Dreever the guard, either. If you do, you'll answer to me.'

Frank Griggs sneered. 'And what would you do, Sheriff? Ride into the pen and tell us off?' Then jerking a thumb in Jake's direction, 'Or maybe you'll be able to raise the dead from the grave! Or maybe you think — '

'Shut up you sick fool!' Jake snapped. 'The only one who is going to have to worry about me, is you! Your sick jokes are getting on this 'killer's' nerves.'

Griggs slumped down on the nearest of the two mattresses and howled in mock fear. 'Ayee! I'm scared to death! Is the big bad killer going to get little old me?' His face contorted into an ugly sneer. 'But maybe you'll find me harder to bump off than an old sleeping man in the night.'

Before Jake could reply, Luke Curren cut in, 'Just shut your mouth, Griggs. I'm going to be riding this caboose with Willie, the guard, here. I've seen the way you like to goad folk and I won't stand for it.' He tapped the wooden butt of his Peacemaker meaningfully. And as Griggs fell silent, he looked at Jake with an almost apologetic expression, as if trying to communicate to the condemned man that he disagreed with the sentence.

Sheriff Dan Foster grinned and

patted his deputy on the shoulder. 'Well said, Luke. I feel comfortable that I'm leaving the prisoners in good hands.'

Luke's eyes lit up. It was clear that he valued the older man's respect.

There was the rap of a cane at the door of the caboose and Judge Anderson poked his head in the entrance. 'Are you ready for the strongboxes, Mr Dreever?' he asked.

The guard crossed the floor and slid the door fully open. Behind the judge stood Zach Harding and eight of his ranch hands. Four of them were lugging a strongbox each, and the other four were cradling Winchesters in their arms.

Sheriff Foster asked, 'This the bank's money, Judge?'

'All safe and sound and ready for loading. It's going back to the head office until they get their act together and send out another bank manager.'

Zach Harding clicked his tongue. 'The wrong decision, I think. Coopersville will be without a bank for however long that takes. How are folks going to conduct their business until then?'

Judge Leroy Anderson rapped his cane irritably on the station boardwalk. 'It was the correct and only logical decision, Zach Harding. It isn't up to the citizens of Coopersville to protect C & L Bank funds. Wilber Sommerton committed suicide and the bank hasn't sent anyone out here. That money is just begging to be stolen and I am not prepared to put the citizenry of Coopersville at any more risk.'

'My boys have kept the money sealed up nice and safe in the bank since the inquest,' returned Zach Harding. 'I could get them to do it for a few days longer.'

'My decision is final!' snapped the judge. 'Now let's get these strongboxes aboard as soon as possible. This money is going back to Logan City where C & L Bank officials will meet the train and collect the load.'

Zach Harding shrugged and instructed his men to load the boxes and stow them in the locked compartment at the other end of the caboose from the cell. Once done they climbed down on to the station boardwalk, as did Sheriff Dan Foster. Baxter Walsh walked along to meet them.

'I will feel happy when that consignment is off SWC property,' he said.

'Which consignment did you mean, Mr Walsh?' asked Dan Foster. 'The bank's gold or my prisoners?'

The railroad chief gave a winsome grin. 'Both, I guess.' He looked up at his guard. 'You ready to go, Willie?'

The old guard smiled down at his boss and opened up the front of his vest, to reveal the butt of a Colt .45. 'I'm ready and raring to go, Mr Walsh. Anything else, or can we get going?'

Walsh shook his head. 'The sooner you get going, the better I'll like it.'

The old guard nodded, stepped down to the platform and drew out a watch from his vest pocket. 'And we're right on time,' he said aloud, pulling out a whistle and raising it to his lips. 'All aboard!' he shouted, waving to Todd

Brodie, the driver, then blowing a shrill blast on his whistle, he mounted the steps of the caboose and swung the great door shut. He pushed the internal bolts in place and leaned out of the shuttered window.

Todd and Chuck had already run a check on their gauges and were waiting for the signal. Todd pulled the steam whistle then clicked the reverser lever into position, released the brake and opened the regulator. Gradually, the Prairie Rose began to chug its way out of the Coopersville station.

Moments after it had left the station Ruby-May Prescott rushed on to the platform, her bosom heaving and with tears running down her cheeks. She stood, a lonely figure, watching the fast retreating train as the rest of the crowd slowly dispersed.

★ ★ ★

The powerful Mogul engine ate up the miles as it hurtled past huge red boulders and stacks, semi-desert with saguaro cactus and scrub, on the long south-west circular route.

Willie Dreever and Luke Curren were sitting playing cards to pass the time. Jake was lying on his mattress with his hands behind his head and his eyes closed, while Frank Griggs stood watching the guard and deputy play cards. He kept up a virtual monologue of jibes, barbs and slights, aimed at all three of his travelling companions.

Luke cast an eye at Jake and saw that his eyes were open. 'Do you mind telling me how you manage to stay so calm, Mr Scudder?' he asked. 'What with — everything?'

Jake yawned, stood up and stretched. He smiled ruefully. 'I guess I've always been an accepting kind of guy. Life's a gamble from start to finish. I've been dealt a raw deal here, but no amount of panicking or squawking about the injustice of it is going to make one whit of difference now. I'll face each thing as it comes, same as I always have.'

Griggs sneered. 'He's a liar, boy! He's quaking in his boots.'

Jake turned to his cell mate and grinned. 'Is that so? Well that must be because I'm in here with you.' Suddenly, his right fist shot out, catching Griggs on the point of the jaw, throwing him back and depositing him on his back on the mattress. Jake stood over him, rubbing his knuckles. 'Funny thing though, you don't seem to scare me at all.'

Frank Griggs felt his jaw, which had immediately started to swell and shot Jake a venomous look. 'Why you — ' he began, as he made to get up.

'Easy now!' warned Luke Curren, himself already on his feet, with his hand on his Peacemaker.

Griggs stayed himself and then flopped back on the mattress and began to laugh. After a moment: 'Reckon I'll let that go, Scudder. Seeing as how it might be one of the last things that you do in the world. Hell, I'm not even going to ask the deputy here to press charges.'

Luke Curren took his hand off his Peacemaker. 'Griggs, you are a truly revolting specimen of a man.'

In answer Frank Griggs merely licked the end of his finger and made a sign on an imaginary board in front of him. 'That's a mark against you then, boy.' He regarded the deputy with an ugly stare. 'I'm a man of my word. I'm coming back sometime to pay off some debts. First I'm going to kill that bastard judge and his pet sheriff. Then maybe I'll come looking for you.'

Luke Curren sat down in the chair and picked up his cards. 'You do that, Griggs. But in the meanwhile just shut up or I'll let Mr Scudder there do what he wants with you.'

'How comes you call him 'mister' Scudder?' Griggs suddenly shouted furiously.

The young deputy smiled. 'Maybe because I have doubts about him being in there with you in the first place.'

★   ★   ★

Beth Lassiter had been reading a book, but had eventually dozed off. She was awakened by the sound of a cough. She opened her eyes to see Norton standing before her with a silver coffee-tray.

'Mr Walsh said I was to look after you, miss. I took the liberty of brewing up some coffee.'

'Thank you, Norton,' she said sitting upright and smiling. 'How long have you been a butler?'

'More years than I care to remember, miss,' he replied, as he poured for her. 'I worked for many of the aristocracy back home then I came to this great land to make my fortune.' He shook his head in the humble manner of one used to being deferential. 'But as you can see, I haven't found it yet. I am still butling. But Mr Walsh is extremely generous. An excellent employer, if I may say so.'

Beth sipped her coffee. 'He has been very generous in letting me travel in his private Pullman.' She looked round at its luxurious trimmings. The desk, the decanters of spirits, the lace curtains and the plush carpets.

'I think he is conscious of the tragedy that you have suffered, miss. Losing your uncle and everything.'

Beth's face clouded. 'I just hate to think of that man being here on this train with us.'

Norton nodded his head. 'But if it's any comfort, miss, it is likely that it will be his last ever train journey.

★   ★   ★

Todd and Chuck were chatting away as they went about their business of maintaining the Prairie Rose. Chuck kept the firebox stoked, and Todd coaxed the great engine along. With only two carriages they were able to hurtle along at a good pace.

'Wonder what the lady will do now?' Todd asked.

Chuck wiped perspiration from his brow. 'Reckon she'll find a Prince Charming and settle down. But you ain't no Prince Charming, loco driver boy!'

'Gah! Take that, you varmint,' Todd returned, aiming a gloved hand at his head. 'You just look after your own business and leave me to mine.' And as the train approached the Horse Neck Bridge he began slowing the engine down to take the bridge smoothly.

'Hey, is that old Clem Brookes on the bridge? He's a good linesman, but he should know better than to be checking the line on the bridge when the Prairie Rose is coming through. I reckon he wasn't expecting us to have made such good time.'

Chuck looked over the side, squinting at the figure on the bridge. 'He's seen us, Todd. He's running for it now,' he said with a grin. 'Give him a blast on the whistle, that'll shift him.'

But before Todd could reach for the whistle pull there was a sudden flash on the bridge and an explosion that sent timber and smoke flying everywhere.

Reflexively, Todd applied the brakes. Then he stared in horror.

As the smoke began to clear a gaping

hole had appeared in the middle of the bridge. 'We . . . we won't be able to stop in time!' Todd exclaimed.

With screeching brakes the Prairie Rose hurtled on, the great engine's stack belching fumes like a dragon. As if in slow motion, it reached the hole and toppled down through the void, twisting as it fell and dragging its two coaches behind it.

The boiler exploded upon impact on the gully floor and a fireball engulfed the mangled engine, whose wheels still turned, churning soil like a massive fire-breathing dragon in its final death-throes. The Pullman and the caboose lay on their sides, wood frames splintered and half-crushed. Steam surrounded the Prairie Rose like an eerie mist.

★　★　★

Jake was aware of someone screaming close by. And then he was aware of pain all over his own body, as if he had been thrown around like a rag doll. He forced his eyes open, immediately squinting as blood trickled into them. He raised a hand and found a gash on his forehead.

'Help me!' cried Luke Curren from somewhere to his left.

Jake was disoriented for a moment. The caboose was in semi-darkness and nothing seemed the way it should have been. Then he recalled an explosion from some way away, a screeching of brakes, being knocked off his feet, turning over and over in the air — then nothing.

He wiped the blood away from his eyes with the back of his hand and allowed his eyes to focus. And the sight that greeted him filled him with horror. The bars of the cell door were no longer vertical, but appeared to be horizontal, and the few pieces of furniture in the main caboose were scattered about what seemed to be the floor, but which he realized was the side wall.

Willie Dreever's face was pressed up against the bars, his eyes sightless and his neck bent at an impossible angle.

Luke Curren was lying on the floor screaming in agony, the cause of which was immediately obvious. The pearly-white but bloody, broken end of his thigh bone was sticking out of a horrific leg wound.

Frank Griggs's voice called to him. 'I'll help you, boy. Throw me the keys!'

Jake felt a spasm of nausea course through him and he doubled over and vomited. As he did so he heard the deputy gasp in agony as he dragged himself across the caboose to where the large bunch of keys had fallen.

'Toss them here, boy, then I'll help,' came Griggs's voice again.

Luke threw the keys towards the cell and a moment later Griggs unlocked the door. 'That's good, boy,' said Griggs, 'now let me take a look at that leg.'

Jake forced back another wave of nausea and looked up to see the young deputy lying on his back, with his Peacemaker grasped in his right hand while Frank Griggs stood over him. 'Easy boy, I just want to look,' said Griggs reassuringly.

Then with a sudden lunge he pushed the ragged end of bone to the side and, as Luke involuntarily fell back, screaming in agony, he casually stepped on the deputy's wrist. 'Sorry about that, Deputy,' he said, leaning down and prising the gun free. 'But I warned you that I keep my promises.' A sadistic leer spread over his face. 'I had an old dog that was in pain once,' he said, ratcheting the hammer of the gun back and lifting the barrel to point directly at Luke's head. 'Putting it out of its misery was the only thing to do.'

Luke began to scream again, but was instantly silenced as the gunshot blew the top of his head off.

Words wouldn't come to Jake's mouth, but he found himself staggering to his feet, ready to launch himself through the doors at Frank Griggs. But

Griggs instantly turned, the gun now squarely aimed at Jake's chest. Having lost his momentum, Jake slumped against the bars of the cell, his breathing laboured. 'Why did you do that? That was coldblooded murder!'

Frank Griggs laughed. 'Yeah, guess it was. And maybe I'm going to do it again in a minute — soon as I find the idiot who set that dynamite off. It wasn't supposed to happen like this.'

★   ★   ★

Beth Lassiter couldn't believe that she was still alive. She was shaken up, her clothes were torn and she had a bump on the side of her jaw, but that was all. She realized that the Pullman carriage was lying on its side in some sort of gully, with steam everywhere. The expensive furniture and trimmings were in shards and shreds.

'Norton!' she exclaimed, her eyes opening in alarm as she saw him push himself to his feet, blood from a

94

laceration on his left ear trickling down on to his white jacket. 'You are hurt. Can I help you?'

But he held a hand up and shook his head silently. 'Oh no, miss,' he said in that curious nasal manner of his. 'But you would assist me if you turned around and put your hands behind your back.'

She stared at him uncomprehendingly for a moment.

He reached inside his white coat and drew out a derringer. His face suddenly hardened and he snapped. 'I said turn round and put your hands behind your back. Now!'

★ ★ ★

Jake stared at the barrel of the Peacemaker. 'Now what? You're going to have a job getting that door open by yourself.'

Griggs merely grinned. 'Oh I reckon we'll be rescued — any second now.'

And as if on cue there was the sound

of boot heels on what now seemed to be the roof of the caboose. 'You all right, Frank?' a voice called out.

'I am, no thanks to whichever fool set off that dynamite. I could have been killed, like two of these no-account scum. You can open the door, the guard and deputy have both cashed.'

The sliding door was rattled but would not budge.

'It's locked from your side, Frank,' the voice outside said plaintively.

With a laugh, Griggs shinned up the cell door, using the horizontal bars like a ladder and slid back the internal bolts. Strong arms reached down and dragged him up. Almost immediately Griggs turned and stood on the edge looking down at Jake. 'Well come on, Scudder, what are you waiting for? Come out.'

Fully expecting a bullet at any moment, Jake climbed out and stood on the side of the caboose facing Frank Griggs. Around them were half a dozen others, two of whom he recognized from his run-in the other day when he had saved Hank Lassiter from them.

'So! It's the dude who crooked my hand,' said a swarthy dark-haired fellow. 'Look Grover,' he said over his shoulder to a youth with a sadistic mouth. 'It's the guy who knocked your hat off and forced you to wear that damned sombrero.'

Grover came forward and without warning lashed out at Jake's head with a left. But despite his grogginess Jake was faster. He ducked back and allowed the blow to sail past him, then he shot forward and landed a straight right to the youngster's midriff. Grover went down, gasping for air.

'That's for taking it out on an old man,' Jake said through gritted teeth.

The men surrounding them laughed and Grover pushed himself up, glowering with rage. His hand strayed towards the gun in its holster, but he was stopped by a barked command from Griggs. 'No time for any of that. Now a couple of you get down there and start bringing up those strongboxes. As for you, Scudder, get down off that caboose and don't move a muscle.'

The men had just brought the last of the boxes out of the caboose and tied them on to horses when Norton appeared from the wreckage of the Pullman, ushering Beth Lassiter ahead of him. She looked both scared and shocked.

'I've got the man who murdered your uncle here, ma'am,' said Griggs, waving his weapon at Jake. 'You want me to kill him?'

She eyed Griggs with revulsion but said nothing.

'You're going to go on a little journey with us,' Frank Griggs went on. Then turning to Norton, he asked, 'Did she give you any trouble?'

'None. It went as smooth as planned — except for this bloody mess!'

Griggs laughed and signalled for the gang to mount up. 'Grover, you take the woman — if you figure you can handle her!'

The youth glowered. 'I can handle her all right.' And with one movement he bent and threw her over his shoulder. Ignoring her shrieks and protestations he tossed her over a saddle and mounted behind her.

Jake glared at Frank Griggs as he languidly mounted the spare horse. 'You won't get away with this, Griggs. So what now? You going to finish it all off by killing me?'

Frank Griggs raised his eyes in mock surprise. 'Kill you, Scudder? Why should I do that? Why, I've even forgiven you for giving me that little tap on the jaw back in the caboose. By the time a posse gets up here they're going to put two and two together and realize that there's a shot deputy sheriff and a convicted killer on the loose. If I were you I'd start running. Just as fast as I could.'

There was the sudden crack of a gunshot and a bullet ricocheted off a small boulder beside Jake. Jake spun round just as Frank Griggs brought his gun up and aimed at the lone figure that had appeared from further along the gully. He recognized Todd Brodie, the train driver. He was standing unsteadily and about to fire again, when Griggs's gun barked out and blood spurted from the side of the driver's head, then he collapsed.

'That's another gun-shot body, Scudder. Better get a move on!'

Jake cursed as he watched Griggs spur his horse after the retreating Marauders gang.

5

Jake found Todd lying face down in the dirt with blood streaming from a head wound. An old Peacemaker lay a few feet away where it had fallen from his hand. He retrieved the gun and shoved it in his waistband, then gingerly turned the train driver over, fully expecting to find him dead.

The punch that caught him on the cheek told him otherwise. He found himself off balance and unready for Todd's follow up that spun him sideways to fall in the dirt. Realizing that to be down was as good as being out of action with this fireball of a driver, he rolled over and came to his feet, just in time to meet Todd's advance with fists flailing.

They traded blow for blow, until Todd threw a haymaker that Jake was able to duck under and charge with his head into his opponent's stomach. They went down together and rolled in the dust before Jake managed to grab the gun from his waistband and claw back the hammer.

'Enough!' he gasped, climbing to his feet with the gun held steady in his hand.

'Go on, pull the trigger,' Todd returned. 'It's empty. I fired my last shot a minute ago.'

The ghost of a smile crossed Jake's now bruised and cut face. He recognized his own ruse of a couple of days before. 'In that case, let's agree a truce.' He held up a restraining hand and handed the gun back. 'We've got to get after those vermin. They've got Beth Lassiter and they killed the deputy. I'm afraid that the guard was killed in the crash.'

'They're both dead?' he asked in horror. Then he thumped his fists together. 'I was afraid of that. And I saw the fight you had with that young bastard and I saw them take Beth Lassiter.'

'Then why did you punch me? I was trying to help. Why did you keep fighting when you saw it was me?'

Todd shrugged. 'You are a condemned murderer. That isn't too good a reputation to have, mister. Besides, when I played possum there I had no idea who was sneaking up on me. For all I knew you could have been getting ready to finish me off.' He put a hand on his jaw and massaged the muscles with his fingers. 'And I was so mad I guess I wanted to hurt somebody. My best buddy was killed in that crash.' His voice quavered. 'He saw us heading for that gaping hole and he pushed me out of the cab. If it hadn't been for him I'd be dead too.' Then his expression hardened and he punched the air in frustration. 'And they've destroyed the Prairie Rose and killed Willie, who was like a pa to me and Chuck. I just wanted to hurt somebody real bad.'

'Todd, I didn't kill Hank Lassiter. I don't know who did, but I believe that

Frank Griggs and the Marauders were behind it.'

'Seeing what I did, I'm inclined to believe you. Maybe we'd better get back to Coopersville and get the sheriff.'

'Are you kidding? It would take forever. We've got to get after them now. They've headed into the Pintos mountains.'

Todd looked up at the telegraph wires which dangled freely. 'The bastards cut the line,' he mused. 'But when the Prairie Rose fails to arrive in Logan City they'll soon try to telegraph back to Coopersville, and when they can't get through they're bound to send out a search party.'

'And when they find this carnage they'll send word to Coopersville. That's all going to take time, Todd. Meanwhile these bastards are getting away.'

'And they've got the girl!' Todd clenched his fists and cursed. 'We have to get her. No telling what men like them would do to her.'

Jake nodded. 'Then we're agreed? We'll get after them.'

Todd's look of grim determination was suddenly transformed into one of immense sadness. 'But first let's do what we need to do for my friends and the deputy. I don't want carrion picking at their flesh.'

★ ★ ★

Beth Lassiter's mind was in turmoil. She couldn't believe all that had happened. Her uncle's death, the train crash and now this! Slung across an outlaw's saddle and being taken who knew where into the Pintos Mountains. Her emotions were bubbling over; a mix of fear, humiliation and almost blind fury. Not only was she extremely uncomfortable, being jostled along with her hands tied behind her back and unable to see much more than the horse's legs, but she had to put up with the outlaw's tuneless whistling and every now and then a slap on her rump with the flat of his hand. At first she had expressed indignation, but ribald laughter from the other members of the column of riders and further slaps had caused her to remain silent. She was all too aware that these men were killers and would consider rape a trivial matter. She willed herself to calm down. If she was to survive, she realized that she would have to be able to think clearly.

After a couple of hours of meandering through a veritable maze of canyons and narrow chasms they came to a valley with a large crudely built cabin and a corral. The men dismounted, unloaded their horses and set about various tasks under the supervision of the man they called Frank Griggs.

'Show the lady to the guest quarters,' he ordered the sarcastic-mouthed youth who had so unceremoniously transported her to this hideout. She felt herself being hauled off the saddle, spun round and then hoisted on to a shoulder again.

'Careful, Grover,' said Frank. 'I can see you need teaching how to handle a lady.'

This remark prompted the outlaw to slap Beth's rump again. 'Damn it, Frank, I know exactly how to handle a woman.'

Griggs laughed. 'Just not yet, Grover. There'll be plenty time later.'

A chorus of ugly laughter confirmed Beth's fears of what the Marauders intended for her. She bit her lip and put up no struggle as Grover took her into the cabin which seemed to be laid out like a bunkhouse. He kicked open a door at the back and tossed her on to a rough bed. She rolled over and glared at him.

'You better not cause any trouble, lady. Not if you want to leave here in one piece.' His mouth twisted into an ugly sadistic leer. 'Makes no difference to me one way or the other.'

★ ★ ★

Jake and Todd buried the three men in shallow graves beside the Prairie Rose, in the full expectation that whichever party that reached the crash scene first would work out what had happened, and that eventually the bodies would be disinterred and taken away for proper burial in consecrated ground.

'We're going to get the vermin who put you three gents in early graves,' Todd pledged, through gritted teeth. He closed his eyes, bowed and made the sign of the cross.

Jake waited a moment until Todd had finished his silent reverie, then: 'But we've got to face it, Todd. We're going to have our work cut out. We're on foot, weaponless except for this old Peacemaker, while they've got horses, a whole arsenal — and Beth Lassiter. I reckon we may need something in the way of a miracle.'

And then he snapped his fingers as he looked towards the Pintos. 'Clem Brookes! Of course. He's a — '

'One of the SWC linesmen. He lives near here, doesn't he?'

Jake clicked his tongue. His momentary elevation of spirits was suddenly dashed. 'But he can't be home now, or else he'd have showed up by now. No one within three or four miles of here could have missed the explosion of that engine.' He shook his head and explained to Todd about his meeting some days before when he and Hank Lassiter had dropped by and Hank had changed his burro team. 'But his place is on the way into the Pintos,' he went on. 'Reckon we should drop by his place and see if we can get hold of some provisions for our trek.'

And they set off, slowly making their way in the heat of the late morning sun. After about half an hour they crested a slight rise and saw Clem's cabin.

'There are still three burros in his corral,' said Jake, taking off his hat and wiping his brow with the back of his hand. 'Two of them look like the two that Hank swapped with him the other day.'

As Todd began to descend towards the cabin, Jake put a restraining hand on his arm. 'It might be a good idea to give him a holler. He was kind of skittish when we visited the other day, and he welcomed us with lead!'

Jake called out Clem's name as they reached the edge of the corral.

Apart from the braying of one of the burros there was no noise.

'Guess he's away from home, like you said,' Todd suggested.

'Then why would he leave his door open?' Jake returned, his eyes narrowing suspiciously. 'We best go in real careful.'

They reached the cabin door unchallenged. Once again Jake called out Clem's name before pushing the door further open with his foot.

The cabin had been trashed and Clem Brookes's battered body was lying on the floor in a pool of his own blood, with a bullet hole in his forehead.

'The bastards were here!' Jake cursed, bending to examine the old linesman, whose hospitality he had enjoyed so recently. He closed Clem's lifeless eyes and stood up, clenching and unclenching his fists in silent rage.

'They beat him up some before finishing him off with a bullet in the brain at close range.'

'What sort of scum are these men?' Todd asked in disbelief. 'Why would they do that?'

Jake shook his head. 'Who knows? But they're building up a tally that needs to be paid for. They've caused the death of four good men so far.'

He picked up the old linesman's Beaumont-Adams Dragoon revolver and the Henry rifle which was propped up against the wall, just as he had seen it the other day. 'At least we've got some sort of ammunition against them now.'

Todd was going through drawers in the rough wooden cupboard behind the door. He pulled out two boxes of shells, one for the Beaumont-Adams and another of .45s, which would fuel the old Peacemaker in his waistband. From another drawer of tools he took out a hand axe and a heavy wood-handled knife. He hefted them alternately in his hands. 'And maybe we'll have to sort of improvise. We aren't exactly a cavalry unit that can go in with bugles blaring and guns blasting.'

Jake took the proffered knife and tucked it in his waistband, and loaded the Beaumont-Adams revolver. 'Those burros are going to prove handy. Can you ride without a saddle?'

'I'll manage,' Todd replied curtly. He nodded at Clem's body. 'But I'm getting real mad at all the graves these jaspers are making me dig.'

★ ★ ★

The rider galloped down the main street and pulled up outside the Excelsior Hotel. Waiting only long enough to tie the reins to the hitching post he entered the hotel at speed, ignoring the girl on the reception desk, and mounted the stairs three at a time. He knocked twice on the door of Baxter Walsh's permanent suite and immediately let himself in.

112

'Norton!' exclaimed the railroad chief. 'What the hell are you doing here? You should be on your way to Logan City with — '

The usually obsequious butler interrupted. 'They blew a hole in the bridge, sir. The train crashed and they — '

'Who are they?' Baxter thundered.

'The Pintos Marauders, sir. They let the prisoners free from the caboose, sir, and they took the strongboxes. Then that Scudder monster, the one the judge sentenced to be hanged, he . . . he killed the deputy and the train driver. He shot them both. I saw it with my own eyes, sir.'

Baxter thumped the desk with his fist. 'The bastards!' Then looking up at his butler: 'What about the Prairie Rose? You said it crashed?'

'It's smashed, sir. It went down the ravine.'

Baxter circled the desk in a few swift steps and grabbed the butler by the shoulders. 'And Miss Lassiter? What about her? Is she dead, too? Out with it man!'

Norton shook his head, his expression becoming pained. 'The gang took her, sir. I thought they were going to kill me too, but they made me come back with a message.' He swallowed hard, as if his mouth had suddenly gone dry. 'They said that if you want to see Miss Lassiter alive again, then no one is to follow them into the Pintos.'

★ ★ ★

Judge Leroy Anderson's face was like thunder and he seemed on the verge of apoplexy as he convened the public meeting in the Coopersville courthouse half an hour later. He had sat listening to Norton's account, and the sheriff's report that the telegraph wires between Coopersville and Logan City had been cut. From time to time he had to call for quiet, but as his own temper rose he just let everyone express their anger. And there was a lot of it. Especially when they heard about the kidnapping of Beth Lassiter.

'We're going to catch the whole danged lot of them,' he finally announced. 'That dog Jake Scudder and the rest of the Pintos Marauders will pay for this outrage. They've blown up a train, stolen the bank's money, murdered four good men and kidnapped Beth Lassiter. We'll hang them one by one right here in Coopersville!'

Cheers and cries of agreement rang round the hall. They quietened down when the tall, commanding figure of the local sheriff stood up and raised his hands for silence. 'We've got to catch them first, Judge. I'm forming a posse here and now, so I want good, fit men to come forward and be sworn in as deputies.'

'You can count me and half a dozen of my men,' said Zach Harding.

'And I'm coming too,' said Baxter Walsh. 'I've got a smashed-up engine lying at the bottom of the Horse Neck ravine, according to my man, Norton. And we've got to get Miss Beth Lassiter free of those swine.'

Norton took a pace forward and coughed in his usual deferential manner before addressing his employer. 'I hope that you won't object to me volunteering to join this manhunt, sir. I have a score to settle with these criminals, and I feel guilty that I let them kidnap Miss Lassiter.'

Baxter Walsh clapped his butler on the shoulder. 'You are a good man, Norton.' Then to the sheriff: 'What do you say, Sheriff Foster? Can Norton come too?'

'I'd be pleased to have him. After what he's been through, and him riding back here and telling us about all this, we owe it to let him have a crack at these vermin.'

The next few minutes were filled with the swearing in en masse of a posse of some twenty men. Judge Anderson had lit a cheroot and was sitting back nodding his head, his high colour of a few moments before beginning to subside now that he saw things were moving.

'You're going to have to set off right away,' he said to Dan Foster.

The sheriff nodded. 'We'll be off as soon as possible.' And then, raising his voice for all to hear: 'I want every deputy to grab some food and drink, then collect some supplies from George Mason's Emporium — which will be paid out of the town's funds — and be ready to follow me in half an hour. We're going to ride as far as we can tonight, maybe even into the night itself. There will be no liquor drinking and no smoking unless I say. This ain't a picnic or any fool turkey hunt. We're going after dangerous men. Jake Scudder is a convicted murderer and has nothing to lose. I want to be bringing every man jack of you back, so you're going to have to be on your toes.'

'And you're going to have a woman jack coming, too!' piped up a lone female voice.

'Ruby-May, what are you doing here?' Judge Anderson asked in surprise, as he and all the rest of the men turned at her entry. 'This is no place for a woman. This is man's work.'

Ruby-May drew herself up and strode into the room, well used to dealing with men in all stages of sobriety and in all moods. She looked up challengingly at Dan Foster. 'I am a citizen of this town, just the same as everyone here. I demand to come along too.'

The trace of a smile crossed Dan Foster's lips. 'You can demand all you want, Ruby-May, but the hard fact is this: I'm the town sheriff in charge of the posse and I decide who comes and who doesn't. I will not take the responsibility of having a woman come along. You're not coming.'

'He's right, Ruby-May,' agreed Zach Harding. 'We're going after that murderer, Scudder. And we've got to get Beth Lassiter out of the hands of the Pintos Marauders. You'd be a liability.'

She turned on him with blazing eyes. 'You all plan to kill him, don't you? Well, I don't believe that Jake Scudder is a murderer. I want to be there to make sure you bring him back alive.'

'What is it with you, Ruby-May?' Dan Foster asked, his eyes narrowing quizzically. 'You only knew the man for what — a few hours of passion, and you believe you know all about him. He's a convicted murderer for — '

Ruby-May's face had flushed the colour of her scarlet gown. She slapped him hard across the face then turned on her heel and flounced quickly out of the hall.

The sheriff stood looking after her. Then he rubbed his jaw and grinned. 'Reckon I touched a raw nerve there.'

Laughter and crude murmurs ran round the hall as everyone started to move out to grab some food and supplies. Yet at least three men in the room were not feeling in any way merry. They all had feelings about Ruby-May Prescott — and every one of them at that moment wished Jake Scudder dead.

6

Jake and Todd had made ground as fast as they could on the burros, but with the failing light it had become increasingly hard to follow the meagre signs the Marauders had left on the hard rock floor of the Pintos canyon network. Periodically, Jake had dismounted the burro that he had christened 'Shifty, on account of his ever-darting eyes,' and knelt down to put an ear to the ground in the vague hope of hearing horses.

'Damn!' he cursed, rising to his feet and quickly remounting. He squinted into the now rapidly failing light. 'We're going to have company soon.'

'A posse?' Todd queried. 'But that's good. We can — '

Jake was shaking his head. 'They'll either hang me right away or pump me full of lead, Todd. I'd best hide while you join up with them.'

Todd stroked his upper lip meditatively. 'Maybe it would be better if we both hid.'

Jake raised his eyebrows quizzically. 'Why both of us?'

'Insurance. I know you aren't a murderer, Jake, and I've no intention of letting anyone let off a stray shot at you. At least if we stay together I can give you some protection.'

Despite his predicament Jake grinned and held out his hand. The two shook as friends.

'Then let's find a place in amongst these boulders and lie low until they pass. I guess two men can move quieter than the army that seems to be following. And hopefully, we'll still have a chance of sneaking up on these Marauder varmints.'

Todd nodded in agreement. 'And rescue Beth Lassiter.'

★　★　★

Dan Foster was having a hard time keeping the members of the posse focused. The problem, as he had soon recognized, was that Zach Harding and Baxter Walsh were both used to giving orders, not taking them.

Blast them! he cursed inwardly, after a further disagreement about which fork to take as they made their way through the maze-like network of canyons and ravines that ran through the Pintos.

With each decision one or the other of them would disagree about his choice of direction. Baxter Walsh had even questioned his ability to read signs.

'There are hardly any signs, damn it!' he had returned, heatedly. 'But I've been a lawman for well nigh fifteen years and tracked dozens of thieves and outlaws. I know how to track, and I know what I'm doing.'

The mutters and murmurs from all the rest of the posse made it clear that the sympathies of the men lay in two directions. It seemed that most of the townsfolk were prepared to back the sheriff's play, while the Lazy H ranch hands and the SWC Railroad men naturally favoured leadership from their bosses.

At last, with darkness upon them, they entered a wide canyon which was bedecked with huge red boulders and stacks.

Sheriff Foster halted his horse and held up his hand. 'We've gone as far as we can tonight, men,' he called as he turned in his saddle. 'We'll bed down and get an early start in the morning.'

And soon, with a fire going and a half-dozen coffee-pots on the go, the posse settled down to a frugal supper and some much needed rest.

After he had figured that all the men had eaten and drunk enough, Dan stood up and addressed them all as they sat or lay on their bed-rolls. 'We'll post a lookout at each end of the camp, for two hour shifts each. I need two volunteers.'

The English butler, Norton, and Zach Harding's ramrod Bill Darby both stood and called out.

'Good men!' He grinned at Norton, as he stood at attention, with his Winchester over his shoulder. 'You're sure used to volunteering, seems to me.' He pointed to a spot about fifty yards back down the canyon beside a group of huge boulders and Norton saluted and ambled past.

'I always like to give good service, Sheriff,' he said as he passed. 'The Duke of Nottingham used to let me look after his gun collection. I know a thing or two about them.'

Dan clapped Bill Darby on the shoulder and pointed to another spot fifty yards down the other end of the canyon. 'If either of you see anything, challenge first then fire a shot and I'll come running.'

Having then sorted out a roster for the subsequent lookouts, the sheriff dowsed the fire with the dregs of a couple of coffee-pots.

'Now settle down everyone,' he ordered. 'I want no talking and the only sound I expect to hear is the soft baby-like snores of twenty plumb-tuckered posse men. Goodnight.'

After a few moments' good-natured banter and the odd mutter of discontent from Zach Harding and his ranch hands, the camp settled down to noisy slumber.

Norton was not at all sleepy, however, despite his lack of sleep over the last day or two. He was peering into the night — waiting expectantly.

He did not have long to wait. Half an hour after the posse had bedded down, a shadowy figure detached itself from the camp and noiselessly made its way over to the butler.

'About bleeding time!' Norton hissed.

'Hold your tongue, you English jailbait! I had to wait until I was sure everyone was asleep.' He was silent for a moment, then, as if in exasperation: 'There's been a change of plan — the Lassiter woman can't leave the Pintos alive.'

Norton blew a soft, almost silent

whistle. 'You want me to tell the gang?'

'Yeah. There's an extra grand for making sure she dies.'

'You can count on me — sir.'

The shadowy figure grunted and then departed back to the camp. Once alone again Norton sat down with his back to a boulder and rolled, then lit a quirly. Deep as he was in his own thoughts, he was unaware that behind the very boulder that he was leaning against were two men who had overheard every word that had been spoken.

★ ★ ★

Judge Leroy Anderson had always had a soft spot for Ruby-May Prescott. Her determination to follow the posse, despite all of the orders from Sheriff Dan Foster, Zach Harding, Baxter Walsh — and himself — had made him realize that a woman with a powerful heat on for a man, just wasn't worth arguing with. It riled him that the man in question was Jake Scudder, a convicted murderer, instead of him, Leroy Anderson, judge for the territory and a prominent and wealthy, unattached local rancher. Yet he had to admire her intent to follow the posse.

He had found her that morning up and dressed in men's range clothes, packing her saddle-bags in readiness to take to the trail.

'I won't let you go, Ruby-May,' he told her.

'Try stopping me, Leroy, and you'll find I'm not the lady you think I am.' She turned to him, arms akimbo, her mouth tight. 'You were wrong, Leroy. You made a bad mistake in finding Jake guilty. You may be a judge, but I'm as good a judge of men as anyone and I'm telling you straight — Jake Scudder is no murderer. You sentenced an innocent man to be hanged.'

'The evidence was overwhelming, Ruby-May,' he told her sternly, as he leaned heavily on his stick. He disliked being brow-beaten by a woman, used as he was to having folks sit and listen to him. But she was a strong woman, and he had a fondness for women of strength. He was aware that it was one of his weaknesses, as witnessed by the way his second wife had upped and run off with a lover and a goodly portion of his wealth.

'Then you are a bigger fool than I took you for, Judge,' she said, equally forcefully. 'I don't know who did kill Hank Lassiter, but I know in my heart it couldn't have been Jake. He — we — got close. A woman can sense things about a man.'

'Are you in love with this killer, Ruby-May?'

'He's no killer! And maybe I am — a bit in love. And that's why I'm going to catch that posse up and make sure there's no lynching. I'm going to bring him back and you're going to re-try him, and acquit him.'

Judge Leroy Anderson shook his head in exasperation and watched helplessly as she slid a Winchester into the boot on her saddle, before hefting the whole rig on to her shoulder.

'Hold it right there, Ruby-May,' he snapped.

'I told you not to try stopping me.'

The judge rapped his stick on the ground. 'Damn it, Ruby-May. I'm saying wait twenty minutes and I'll get my stuff and saddle up, too. I'm coming with you.'

* * *

Jake and Todd had spent a wretched night behind the boulder, unable to get back to their burros because of their proximity to the succession of lookouts. Using only basic sign-language they agreed to take turns to doze while the other kept a wakeful ear for any movement of the posse lookout. It was only at daybreak when the rest of the posse roused and the lookouts rejoined them that they managed to slip back to the place where they had tethered the two burros.

'It's just as well that you stopped me last night, Jake,' Todd whispered. 'I would have throttled the life out of that butler bastard. He's been in on this thing from the very start.'

Jake nodded. 'And now we know that there's a link between some of the posse and the Pintos Marauders.'

'But who was that guy?'

Jake shrugged his shoulders. 'I thought the voice was familiar, but I hardly had time to get properly acquainted with anyone in Coopersville.'

Except for Ruby-May, he thought wistfully. And before he knew it he was thinking of her and what might have been if they had only had more time. But maybe there could still be time, he thought as he gritted his teeth determinedly.

And then to Todd: 'I guess we'd better follow them at a distance.'

Just then they became aware of raised voices from the camp. Gingerly, they peered between the rocks and saw a heated argument taking place between the sheriff, Baxter Walsh and Zach Harding. A few moments later it became apparent that the posse had split in two, one faction mounting up and heading off with the sheriff, the other heading off with the rancher and the railroad boss.

'A bust up!' mused Todd. 'That poses us a dilemma. Do we follow one group each or take pot luck and stick together?'

Jake chewed his lip for a moment, then shook his head. 'Neither. I think we should split up too. And I reckon I'm going to let this burro do what it does best and climb up on to that rimrock and see if I can skitter across the tops. That way I may be able to get a sight of the Marauders' camp.'

Todd nodded in agreement. 'Sounds sensible, as long as you stay out of sight of the two posses. As for me, I figure I'll tag along behind the half posse that's got Norton in it.'

They shook hands before they mounted their burros. 'One of us will get her,' Jake said.

'We'd better,' returned Todd, his face grim.

★ ★ ★

The sun beat down unmercifully as Todd followed the half posse that was led by Zach Harding and Baxter Walsh, through the maze of the Pintos canyons.

'These guys have no idea where they're going!' he mused to himself. 'I reckon we've probably either circled the Marauders once or twice or we're dozens of miles astray. We'll probably be here all week.'

And as he said it he was aware of his stomach rumbling. He had eaten almost all of the meagre supplies they had been able to assemble from the old linesman's cabin. 'Looks like this last bit of bread is going to have to last a long time, eh burro?' He leaned forward and scratched the animal's head between its ears and it responded with a vigorous shake of the head. 'Well at least we've got water. Did I ever tell you how much water the Prairie Rose needs to — ?'

He stopped talking and a lump came into his throat as the thought of his beloved engine and his dead friends suddenly hit him with the force of a battering ram. And then he saw Beth Lassiter in his mind's eye and his emotions turned in a different direction. Then he was overwhelmed with fear for her safety.

He thumped his thigh. 'For God's sake, Todd Brodie,' he rebuked himself. 'You've barely even spoken to the woman — how can you think you're in love with her!'

A moment later he had to stop his burro as he saw a member of the distant posse hang back, then edge his horse behind an outcrop of rocks.

'That's Norton!' he whispered to the burro, used as he had become to confiding in the animal. 'Now we're talking. You just go your own way, Mister Fancy English butler — I'm going to be tailing you from now on.'

And as Norton made off in another direction from the retreating posse, Todd forced back the urge to catch him up and beat him to a pulp. First things first, he thought. Let him lead me to the outlaw hide-out — then I'll settle with him.

★ ★ ★

It was afternoon by the time that Judge Anderson and Ruby-May reached the scene of the Prairie Rose crash. The great engine lay blackened and charred, with the smashed-up Pullman and caboose lying on their sides behind it.

'The posse came through here, all right,' said the judge, pointing to the multitude of hoof prints. He rode along the length of the train and pointed sadly at the three graves. 'I guess they took time to bury those poor men.'

Ruby-May rode alongside him. She shook her head. 'I doubt it, Leroy. The posse were in such a rush last night that I guess they barely stopped here.'

'So who buried them?'

'Well it would hardly have been the outlaws, would it? It was someone with a decent streak.'

'Meaning who, Ruby-May?'

'I mean it was probably Jake.'

Judge Anderson snorted contemptuously. 'Ruby-May, you're blind as far as that man is concerned. What did he do to you? Put a hex on you or something?'

Ruby-May blushed. 'Judge, you can rant all you want, but I have an idea what happened here. Maybe it's woman's intuition, but I know where I'm going now.'

The judge removed his hat and wiped his bald brow. 'You've got me mystified. Where are you going to go?'

She turned her horse and began to ride off. 'I'm following my intuition, Judge. You go wherever you want.'

Judge Anderson was used to giving orders and he was not pleased to be treated in such an off-handed manner. He pulled out a cheroot from an inside pocket of his coat and struck a light to it. A fox-like gleam appeared in his eyes and he blew out a satisfied stream of blue smoke.

'Hold on, Ruby-May,' he called, spurring his mount forward. 'I think I know where you're headed. I'll come along — just in case you need my protection.'

★   ★   ★

In the fading light of the evening, after a gruelling day of riding, Jake blessed his little burro and patted its neck as he looked down from the rimrock and saw a large crudely built clapboard cabin below. He counted about a dozen horses in the corral adjacent to it.

'You've done a good job, Shifty,' he whispered. 'We've found them. Now all I have to do is reconnoitre the place. Guess I'll wait until dark and do it on foot.'

An hour later he started down a rough trail on foot, having left Shifty tethered on a tangle of scrub-oak, happily munching away on some rough grass. It was not an easy descent, but he was able to see well enough by the light of the moon. And as he went, he committed the path he took to memory.

When he reached the foot of the canyon he started edging his way towards the cabin. Then suddenly, he felt the unmistakeable nozzle of a handgun in the small of his back.

'Stop right there, pilgrim,' a voice barked at him. 'Looks like you've found a pathway straight to your Maker!'

7

Most of the Marauders had been drinking rot-gut whiskey for several hours and were starting to get restless. Frank Griggs had been watching them and reading the signs. It was never an easy matter to keep a dozen outlaws under control. Mostly he managed it through sheer dominance, by making them all believe that he was capable of killing any of them with no more thought than he would grind a bug underfoot. But this business was different. They were playing for high stakes, enough maybe to take him out of this outlaw life, perhaps enough to disappear and show up someplace far away and buy a little spread of his own. But the rest of the Marauders didn't know anything about this. They thought that they had the bank money and they had the girl, and that they'd be able to make money out of her by holding her to ransom. That was why he'd let them start drinking, so that they could celebrate.

But now, as he sat smoking a quirly and sipping coffee laced with whiskey, he judged that the time had probably arrived to introduce some other diversion. Not all of them were dim-witted dregs and cut-throats. Some like Manson and Grover had enough brains to work out why they were just sitting it out in their secondary hideout.

He shrugged as he made a mental decision. What did it matter if they roughed the woman up a bit? The boys needed a distraction.

'Grover, pass me that deck of cards,' he called.

Grover languidly rose from his chair and picked up the well-used deck of cards from the meal table and handed them to the outlaw boss. 'You planning to play a little solitaire, Frank? Or do you plan something more dangerous?' He grinned. 'Maybe you want us to play a little poker to increase or decrease our shares in all this gold we stole?'

Frank casually drew on his quirly and blew a slow stream of smoke ceiling-wards. He grinned back, smugly aware that he had judged Grover's intellect correctly. The young man was getting impatient.

'Listen up, you Marauders,' he called out, immediately claiming the gang's attention. 'I thought we'd have a little game — for those of you that haven't drunk too much! We've got a little lady in that room next-door who's sure bound to be bored with sitting around all day. How about we entertain her?'

'Now you're talking, Frank.'

'Thought you'd got her planned for yourself!'

Other ribald and uncouth comments followed, and Frank milked them for all they were worth. He shuffled the cards, squared them up then deliberately placed them down on the floor in front of him.

'OK. Here's the deal. We cut the deck in age order. Lowest card wins. Aces low. Any same card draws will cut again to decide who goes first.'

He smiled as he watched their lust rise. 'And just so you all know: I'm a fair man and will take my turn according to Lady Luck.' Slowly, he untied his bandanna and slid it off his neck. 'But as boss of this outfit I claim a right — '

With an ugly leer he grasped an end of his bandanna in each hand and tugged them taut, then continued, 'I claim my right to also have her last!'

★   ★   ★

Jake had stiffened the moment he had felt the gun in his back. He reflexively raised his hands.

'Well, well, it's Jake Scudder, isn't it?'

'That's me,' Jake replied. 'And your name is Manson, isn't it?'

'That's right, and I still owe you for giving me this hand wound. It hurts a lot. How do you think I ought to repay you?'

'By letting me go?' Jake responded in a deliberately whimsical tone.

The gun was jabbed roughly into his back. 'You ain't funny, pilgrim. I guess the best I can do is to let you live long enough to see Frank. And Grover, of course. He's feeling a tad revengeful about that roughing up you gave him back at the train crash.'

'Yeah, you boys really botched that up, didn't you? Almost killed Frank Griggs! But you and Grover are a real pair of botchers, aren't you? Cowardly ones too!'

'You're a real funny man, ain't you Scudder.'

'Better than being a coward. It was you and him that beat up and murdered old Clem, the linesman, wasn't it?'

'We only softened the old fool up. We didn't kill him. That was — '

'Frank Griggs! Thought so,' Jake returned, goadingly. 'But I reckon you'll hang for your part in his murder.'

Manson pulled back the hammer of the gun. 'And I reckon I won't let you live after all. I'll tell Frank that you — '

'Yeah, he's going to think you were real smart, firing off a shot to bring the posse about your ears.'

Jake felt the pressure of the gun nozzle slacken, then disappear. And in that instant he dodged to the right and spun round. He saw Manson's gun arcing downwards as the outlaw attempted to pistol whip him. He felt a momentary spasm of pain as the butt of the gun skidded off his left shoulder, but in almost the same action his right hand came up, balled into a fist and smashed into Manson's solar plexus. The outlaw doubled up and Jake's left knee came up sharply to meet his jaw. He immediately followed it up with a straight right that hurled the outlaw backwards, his head connecting with a rock with a sickening thud. His lifeless body slid to the ground.

Jake made sure that he was dead then

dragged his body into a patch of scrub. Then buckling on Manson's gunbelt and checking the heft of the Navy Colt that so recently had threatened to blow his spine apart, he repositioned Clem Brookes's old Beaumont-Adams revolver in his waistband then set about checking the place out. He heard the noise coming from the cabin, but decided first of all to explore a small shack that seemed to be built onto the crude wooden privy-closet that had been erected a wholesome distance away from the cabin.

As he expected it was a sort of store containing a supply of tins, oil lamps, candles — and two sticks of dynamite.

Jake picked the dynamite up and kissed it. 'Reckon you could be pretty darned useful,' he mused. 'Now my main job is to find Beth Lassiter.'

★　★　★

Beth had barely eaten all day, having refused the trays that had been given to

144

her. But she had drunk the coffee, determined as she was to stay awake, to deal with whatever the outlaws were prepared to throw at her.

The evil-eyed youth called Grover opened the door and entered. He was grinning maliciously and holding a playing card in his hand.

'Looks like I won you first,' he said. His voice was slightly slurred, as if he had suddenly consumed a large quantity of whiskey. 'I told you that you'd better be nice.'

Beth stared at him in horror. 'Wh-what do you mean, you won me?'

'I'm first!' He took a pace towards her. 'Now how about a little kiss to start?'

Beth was on her feet, starting to back away. 'Stay away from me, you monster.'

'Playing hard to get, huh?' And he ran at her.

Beth screamed and dodged him. She ran across the crude bed. She looked wildly round the room, but it was

145

useless. She already knew that there was nothing whatever for her to defend herself with. The Marauders had seen to that.

'Make as much noise as you want, honey,' Grover sneered. 'There ain't nobody going to come in to help you.' A coarse chuckle escaped from his throat. 'Besides, you're going to meet all the boys later — personally!'

He rushed her and pinned her arms by her sides, drawing her to him so suddenly that she had no opportunity to knee him in the groin, as she had been planning to do.

But she did manage to bite his lower lip when he tried to press his mouth on hers.

'Bitch!' he exclaimed, releasing her immediately and putting a hand to his bleeding lip. Then he dealt her a vicious back-handed slap across the face that sent her reeling. As she tottered backwards, he shoved the flat of his hand into her face and pushed her roughly back on to the bed.

'Don't come near — ' she breathed, but was silenced by a heavy swipe to her left temple.

'You better learn to be nice, woman!' he grated at her. 'There are a lot of men waiting out there, and most of them are a whole lot less polite than me.'

Beth stared in horror as he straddled her and began to unbuckle his belt.

★　★　★

Baxter Walsh and Zach Harding were not far off coming to blows.

'We've wasted another damned day with all this circling around these canyons. How come we started out without some sort of a map?' Walsh demanded.

'There is no darned map,' returned Zach. 'These mountains and canyons are pretty well uncharted. That's what makes them ideal for scum like the Marauders.'

'Well, we're no nearer catching them than we were yesterday.' He looked up at the moonlit sky, which periodically darkened even more as clouds scudded across the moon. 'We're going to have to make camp soon.'

Zach Harding scowled. The railroad boss was right, he knew, but he hated having his men hear and think that he was taking an order from anyone.

'We can't stop yet. There's another half-hour or so of riding that we can do by moonlight. Besides, have you forgotten why we're here? Those men have got Beth Lassiter. We have a duty to get her.'

'As well as catching that Scudder bastard,' Baxter agreed.

And as he said it they both realized that when they did catch Jake Scudder his fate would be sealed quickly. They both knew what that would do to Ruby-May Prescott. She was besotted with Scudder for some reason. She would not be pleased with either of them.

And both of them badly wanted Ruby-May to like them.

The Marauders were drinking even more and becoming ever more ribald. They clapped and hooted with glee when they heard Beth's scream and the ensuing squeal of pain from Grover, followed by cursing and the sounds of several blows on flesh.

'Maybe that boy does know what to do with a woman, after all,' one of the older outlaws jibed, as they talked among themselves about the train crash and the robbery.

'You're all going to be rich men when we share out this hoard,' Frank Griggs said. 'For now let's all just enjoy our little entertainment.'

One of the men who had not been drinking much suddenly took to his feet. 'I don't believe that Grover does know how to handle a woman!' He thumped his fist on the wall. 'What the hell are we playing at here, Frank? That's a good-born woman in there with Grover, not some dollar whore.

Why are you allowing her to be raped? What sort of a gang have we become?'

'We've become the men we are because of fair-born women like her,' Griggs returned cryptically. 'You getting squeamish, Tallisker?'

'Darned right I'm getting squeamish! I don't hold with violence to women. What do the rest of you say? Let's stop this right now. I agree we should ransom the woman, but we shouldn't harm a hair on her head.'

For the most part he was shouted down.

'Come on, Red,' the man called Tallisker said appealingly to an older man whose name derived from his ruddy complexion.

'I dunno, Tallisker,' said Red, hesitantly looking at Frank Griggs and the rest of the bleary-eyed, whiskey-fuelled Marauders.

Frank Griggs laughed. 'What's the matter, Tallisker? Do you have so many lady friends that you can pass up on a little fringe benefit?'

'This isn't funny, Frank. I'm going to put a stop to it right now!'

'I wouldn't do that if I were you, Tallisker. You've been reading that Bible of yours too much.'

'At least I've got some sense of decency,' Tallisker returned. He took three paces towards the door to the room, then suddenly threw his arms out as a knife thumped into his back. He made a gasping noise, rocked on his feet for few moments then pitched forward on his face and lay still.

The Marauders went silent. Violent men though they were, even the most hardened one had been taken by surprise at the sight of one of their number being skewered in the back.

Frank Griggs's laugh rang eerily through the room. He stood up and walked casually over to the prone body of the dead outlaw. He retrieved his knife and wiped the blade on Tallisker's back. 'I can't abide a spoilsport,' he said jocularly. 'Now a couple of you drag this carcase out of here. I don't want to have to put up with seeing him bleeding all over the place. Anyone who wants can have his belongings, and his share of the gold will go into the total pot.'

Two of the gang, one of them the ruddy-complexioned man called Red, instantly sobered, through a mixture of fear and shock. They grabbed an ankle each and began dragging the body towards the cabin door.

But they didn't reach it. The door was suddenly kicked open and an eight inch stick with a sizzling fuse arced through the air from the darkness outside, bounced once and lay smoking and sparking on the floor between the Marauders and the door.

'Enjoy your trip to hell, you bastards!' cried a voice from outside, and the door was pulled shut.

8

The Marauders stared in speechless horror at the rapidly burning fuse, no one knowing what to do. And then panic broke out, as the realization of imminent death dawned upon them. Red and the other outlaw dropped Tallisker's legs and started shuffling backwards, as did the rest of the gang.

'Get that damned door open!'

'It's going to blow any second!'

But the door had been bolted from outside and would not budge.

Only Frank Griggs had the presence of mind to head towards the sizzling dynamite stick. He stomped a boot hard on the wildly sparking fuse and, reaching down to grasp the stick, yanked it hard to pull the fuse off.

'Thank God, Frank,' Red gasped. 'Who the hell — '

But Frank Griggs was staring down

at the stick in his hand, now detached from the sparking fuse on the floor. A slow smile spread across his features and he grinned.

'It isn't a dynamite stick,' he said, raising it up for the Marauders to see. 'It's just wood.' And he tossed his head back and began to laugh.

★ ★ ★

Beth was determined that she would not submit to rape while ever she was conscious and capable of some sort of retaliation. She bit, scratched and attempted to gouge at Grover's eyes. But he had finally overpowered her with a couple of punches to the side of her head which left her groggy. Then he pinioned her wrists above her head with one hand and began to haul his britches down with the other.

The drunken shouting from the room next-door only vaguely impinged upon Beth's consciousness. The hammering at the door that followed merely drew a string of invective from Grover.

'I ain't ready!' he shouted. 'I'll tell you when you can — '

The explosion suddenly blew in the side wall of the cabin. Beth gasped as the force of the fire and smoke ball threw Grover on top of her, squeezing the air out of her lungs. For a moment she felt as if she had been both deafened and blinded and all she could do was fight for air in the seething heat. But with every breath she only seemed to take in smoke and she coughed and began to retch. Then she became aware of the outlaw's sheer weight pinning her to the bed.

And then she heard him scream, and as her vision cleared, she saw flames engulfing his back, and several large splinters of wood protruding from his back and neck. Blood was starting to flow from his awesome burns and wounds. Despite her loathing for him she shivered at the agony that he undoubtedly was in.

Then suddenly, it was as if he had

been lifted and dragged off into the fire and smoke of hell. Strong hands hauled her to her feet and before she knew it she was tossed across the powerful shoulders of a man who turned and darted through the gaping hole in the cabin wall. Unable to do anything but cough and retch she felt herself being jostled up and down as her rescuer ran. Then she was tossed across the back of a horse.

'Don't move a muscle, ma'am,' a voice snapped at her. 'I've just got to light this.'

She saw the flare of a match and a moment later heard the sizzle of a fuse being ignited.

And then from the cabin she heard men shouting and guns being fired.

Her vision was only just reverting to normal. She blinked hard and saw the sparkling stick of dynamite arc through the air and land on the ground thirty or forty feet away near the cabin entrance — then explode.

Her rescuer sprang up behind her

and immediately urged the horse on. As he did so he spun round and let off a fusillade of shots from a handgun. They departed into the moonlight amid a hail of returned fire from the outlaws.

Just as the horse was lengthening its stride, it let out a strange moaning sound and seemed to falter, as if it had taken a stray bullet.

'Damn!' the man cursed. 'That was what I was most afraid of.'

★　★　★

Todd's temper was rising to boiling point as he kept a respectable distance between him and Norton, his quarry. It was getting dark and despite the moonlight he had closed the gap as much as he dared. His hunger had been mounting and his muscles had seemed to progressively stiffen. For a man used to riding the footplate rather than on horseback, far less on a burro, he was discovering aches in muscles he hadn't realized that he had. And with the monotony of following the Englishman, he alternately blamed Norton and the burro that had carried him so far.

''Course I'm only joshing,' he whispered to the burro, tickling it between its ears as he did so. 'You're no Prairie Rose, that's for sure, but I reckon you've got the same kind of heart as she did. You just keep puffing away. I reckon she'd have taken to you.' He stopped and dismounted to ease the discomfort in his rear.

'That Norton sure knows where he's headed,' he mused, as he watched the slowly advancing man on his horse. They had made their way unfalteringly through the network of canyons and ravines. 'Makes a change from following the posse, with all its doubling back and hesitating over which way to go. I reckon he's taking a route to avoid them, all of which means that he knows the Pintos pretty damned well.'

As he squinted into the darkness he remounted the burro and urged it after the so-called butler. 'Wonder if he even is an Englishman?' he mused. And with a grin he said to the burro, 'Reckon I'm going to enjoy showing him where you can put a tray.'

The burro snickered, as if it saw the joke.

From somewhere in the distance there came the sound of an explosion, followed after a few moments by another.

★   ★   ★

The noise of the explosions had echoed and reverberated through the canyon system for miles and created many false impressions as to their source. And frustratingly, that was precisely what Sheriff Dan Foster was being inundated with as each and every member of his half posse expressed an opinion to him as to the nature of the explosions and the direction from which they came.

'The bastards have blown themselves up!'

'They've blasted half a mountain to

stop us following them.'

'We need to go this way, Sheriff.'

'No, that way.'

Dan Foster scratched his jaw and inwardly cursed at the number of opinions expressed.

'Pipe down, all of you!' he exclaimed after a moment. 'It's dark and we're not going to fall into any kind of a trap. We're not going to go blustering in anywhere. Now gather round me, I'll tell you exactly what we're going to do.'

* * *

Ten miles away Zach Harding and Baxter Walsh were faced with a similar situation with their half posse. But since more of the posse were composed of Zach Harding's Lazy H hands there was far less discussion. They went the way Zach Harding thought they should go.

'OK, but it's your funeral,' said Baxter Walsh.

'And maybe your's too,' returned the rancher. 'But we'll go this way!'

* * *

The horse lost speed, but managed to keep going and carried Beth and her rescuer out of the reach of the handguns. But it was faltering with each step that it took and it seemed inevitable that they would be caught as soon as the outlaws gained their horses. It therefore puzzled Beth that her rescuer continued to let off shots from his gun, despite the fact that he couldn't possibly hit any of the outlaws.

And then he abruptly yanked on the reins and changed direction so that they were moving at right angles up an incline. The horse struggled and finally collapsed, tossing them off and lying on its side gasping.

To her horror the man immediately put the muzzle of his gun to the animal's head and fired two shots.

'You . . . you . . . ' she began, but was immediately silenced by a hand that was cupped over her mouth and she found herself half-shoved, half-dragged

161

up the rest of the incline.

'Shush! Not a word!' he urgently warned in a soft voice, inexplicably letting off another round.

When they reached the top of the incline he pulled her against a rock face as they heard the sound of several horses racing past in the moonlight.

'I think they bought it,' he said. 'I couldn't afford to let them hear that horse breathing its last.'

'My God, you think fast, Mr — whoever you are.'

Her rescuer said nothing for a moment, then: 'Scudder, ma'am. Jake Scudder — not that we've ever been properly introduced.'

Beth felt her face suffuse with heat and her mind seethe with conflicting emotions. She had felt unbelievably relieved and grateful to this man for rescuing her from a fate worse than hell, yet as he told her his name she began to feel a surge of fury.

'You killed my uncle! You . . . you — ' she exclaimed. And before she knew it she had lashed out with the flat of her hand, dealing him a stinging slap across his face.

Scudder barely flinched. He had expected some such reaction. 'No ma'am, I didn't kill Hank Lassiter. We were all set to become good friends. Trouble seemed to have latched on to him the day we met and I actually saved him three times that day.'

'I had heard that,' Beth admitted. 'But what are you saying? That you were framed? That someone else murdered my uncle and tried to put the blame on you?'

'That's exactly what I'm saying, ma'am. But I don't know who it was — yet! Except that the Marauders are all involved in it. That train robbery was not a simple act to get hold of the gold. There was more to it than that.'

'I worked that out myself.' She shivered. 'Those men were monsters. They were planning — '

'I saw what they were planning, ma'am. Todd Brodie, the train driver, survived the crash as well. He and I managed to hide from the posse and we overheard that dog Norton talking to someone.' And he gave her a brief account of all that he knew and of how he had managed to come over the tops on the burro, while Todd had tailed Norton the butler.

'But the reason we split up was so that one of us could rescue you. And not just from being raped, ma'am. Whoever was behind all this has ordered that you were to be killed.'

Despite herself Beth gasped in horror.

'And that's why we've got to get moving. Those men will probably chase shadows for a few miles, but I reckon they'll be forced to turn back soon.'

'So what shall we do? Do we need to go back and get another horse?'

Jake shook his head. 'That's too risky. I've got a friend just up on the rise here. The best danged burro in the territory. We'll get him and make our way out of the Pintos.'

She put a hand on his arm as they started up the rise. 'I'm sorry, Mr Scudder. I haven't thanked you.'

He patted her hand. 'Let's just get out of here in one piece.'

★ ★ ★

Frank Griggs raised his hand and brought the Marauders to a halt.

'It's no good in this light,' he growled. 'We've lost them — for now. We'd better head back, get a few hours' rest until sunup, then we'll hunt them down.'

'Don't you think we should try a little longer, Frank?' the outlaw called Red urged.

'I said we'll try at sunup. Besides, we don't want to go running into a posse do we?'

And the rest of the Marauders agreed with this irrefutable logic. None of them fancied walking into an ambush. Or even worse, risking getting caught and ending up with a noose round their neck.

★ ★ ★

Norton had been puzzled when he heard the explosions. He assumed that they had come from the outlaw camp and that they were due entirely to the Marauders. He could picture them getting drunk, and then some fool like Manson or Grover lighting a stick of dynamite just for the hell of it.

'Dumb fools,' he muttered to himself 'They're a couple of real lowlife scum. They enjoyed hurting people and destroying things just for the hell of it. Good thing the posse is made up of fools who couldn't find their way home on a dark night. Still, even a bunch of numbskulls might get lucky and stumble across the right way into the number two camp, especially when idiots are setting off dynamite.'

Then for a moment he wondered whether they'd tried to dynamite open the strongboxes. But he discounted this thought almost immediately.

'Not even they could be that stupid!'

Always a cautious man he took his time covering the rest of the journey in the fading moonlight.

Not long afterwards, he was surprised to find himself able to approach the hideout without being challenged by a lookout. And as he came nearer, the unmistakeable smell of dynamite and burnt wood was all too obvious.

There was a light on in the main room of the cabin, but half the wall had been blown away. The corral was empty and there appeared to be no one about. He rode up to the corral, dismounted and drew his gun, just in case.

It was then that he heard someone moaning, as if in great pain. He advanced to the gaping hole that had once been the cabin wall, and saw Grover lying face down on the floor, his clothes literally burned away and with four or five large spikes of wood protruding from his back. He was lying in a pool of his own blood.

'Norton!' Grover wheezed. 'Need — water — need help.'

167

The butler knelt down beside his fellow gang member. 'You all alone, Grover? They all gone and left you?'

'Please — water! The pain — agony.'

Norton winced at the sight of the wooden spikes embedded in his back. 'Well, you've handed out enough pain to others, haven't you? Seems like poetic justice that you should die in agony too.'

Grover attempted to push himself up, his pain-wracked body shaking with the effort to do so. 'Norton, get me — water!'

Norton sucked air between his lips. 'Ah, you see, I don't like that. Everyone thinks that because I do this butling thing, they can order me about. But I've had enough of all that, you see. I'm not going to obey orders like that any more. No sir, soon I'm going to have enough money to buy me some servants of my very own.'

'Norton! You can have — my share — I'm begging you — '

'That's better, Grover,' he returned. 'But I still don't think I can do much for you. Looks like you're going to die.' He suddenly beamed as he reached down and grabbed a handful of hair and yanked the outlaw's head back. 'The least I can do is put you out of your misery.'

Grover frantically struggled to free himself. But it was in vain. Norton grabbed his head and twisted sharply. There was a cracking noise, like a stick breaking and Grover's body instantly went limp.

The butler dropped his head and then patted the dead outlaw on the shoulder. 'Don't mention it, old chap,' he said. 'It was a pleasure.'

He stood up and dusted himself down, suddenly aware that he was hungry. 'Let's see if there's anything to eat around here,' he mused. 'Killing gives a man an appetite.'

*   *   *

When the Marauders arrived back at the camp half an hour later, Norton was sitting at the main table mopping up a plate of beans with a corn tortilla and sipping a mug of Arbuckles coffee.

'I see you've had some sort of adventure, Frank,' he commented casually, as the outlaw leader came in and helped himself to coffee. The others tossed themselves on bunks and were soon dozing noisily.

'And I see that Grover and Tallisker have both bought it,' he added. 'I put their bodies together. Didn't want to spoil my appetite by having to look at Tallisker.'

'Didn't know that Grover had cashed,' Griggs replied with little interest. 'I'm guessing that we'll also find Manson's remains at first light when we head off again.'

Norton stopped with his mug halfway to his mouth. 'Why are you breaking camp? The boss didn't give any such order.'

Frank Griggs's eyes narrowed and he snapped, 'I have no boss, Norton! You'd do well to remember that.' He swallowed a mouthful of coffee and laid his mug down while he rolled a quirly. 'And we ain't breaking camp. We're going after some property that was stolen.'

Norton stiffened. 'The gold?'

Griggs shook his head and lit his quirly. 'The girl. Some clever bastard suckered us and stole her away.' He grinned maliciously. 'Just when the evening was starting to get interesting. But we'll catch up with them after sunup. They won't get far at night. Then they'll pay — in full!'

Norton nodded, then told Griggs about the posse splitting in two, and the new 'orders' he had been told to convey to Griggs.

'So the woman mustn't leave the Pintos alive,' he finished.

'That's kind of what I had in mind anyway,' Griggs replied, blowing a plume of smoke from the corner of his mouth. 'After we've had some fun.'

'And does that fun include killing this rescuer of hers?'

'Of course! You want to be in on that, Norton?'

'I'd prefer not to,' he said, deliberately putting on a pained expression. 'I'm a tad squeamish that way, Frank. I've hardly slept and I'm dog-tired. What say you if I just stay here and look after the gold.'

Frank Griggs stubbed his quirly out and grinned. 'Hell no! I wouldn't expect an English butler to do any real work. Of course, if you have any idea of disappearing with these strongboxes that we have here, well, just put it out of your mind right now. The fact is that the last man who double-crossed me actually lived long enough to see me pull his bowels out of the gut wound I gave him.'

Norton visibly paled. 'Loyalty has always been one of the most desirable qualities of a butler, Frank. You can depend on me.'

And as Frank Griggs retired to his bunk, Norton glared at his back.

Yes, sir, he thought malevolently, if either of us is going to do any disembowelling around here, it's going to be me, not you, Frank Griggs!

9

Judge Leroy Anderson had fantasized about Ruby-May over several years. They had enjoyed a sort of relationship that was more than the usual saloon owner and client relationship, and more than just being fellow poker players. But it was far from the intimacy that he craved with her. Yet going off together and being forced to share the night in relative comfort had given him some hope.

After a frugal meal, and with a couple of whiskies down them, Ruby-May unexpectedly opened her heart to him.

'I can't help my feelings, Judge,' she confessed, shaking her head and taking a hefty swallow of whiskey. She looked up, beamed affectionately at him and raised her glass to him. 'You are a good man, Leroy Anderson. I've always liked you . . .'

The judge was in the process of lighting a cheroot, but at her hesitation he stopped with the match halfway towards it. He gulped, then: 'You've always liked me, Ruby-May? In what way?' he asked hopefully.

'Like a father!' She tilted her head slightly and beamed again. 'You're like the father I wished I could have had.'

Judge Anderson stared at her for a moment too long, for the match suddenly burned his fingers and he dropped it, and the cheroot fell from his mouth.

'Damn! Damn!' he exclaimed, blowing on his fingertips and jumping to his feet.

Ruby-May couldn't prevent herself from laughing, and at the sight of her the crusty old judge began to loosen up. He let out a guffaw, then before long they were both in the grip of hysterics.

'God almighty!' said Ruby-May at last. 'I haven't had a thing to laugh about for days.' She shook her head and her brow suddenly creased with worry. 'I don't rightly understand what's happened to me — except I believe that I'm in love.'

The judge had just retrieved his cheroot. 'In love?'

Ruby-May nodded. 'With Jake Scudder.' She held up a hand. 'I know what you'll say to that. You'll tell me that I hardly know him. But none of that seems to matter. There's just a kind of magic that happened between us, and I believe that he feels the same way too.'

She reached over and squeezed his knee.

'You'll help me, won't you Judge?'

Leroy Anderson patted her hand and struck another match to light his cheroot.

Oh I'll help you all right, he mused to himself. I'll cure you of this madness — by hanging that murdering dog, Jake Scudder!

* * *

Jake and Beth had made their way along the ridges and rimrocks by the light of the moon. After her ordeal of the last couple of days Beth had soon fallen asleep and dozed as Jake led the burro along the narrow, undulating trail. By sun-up Jake was just about dead on his feet, but he was ever conscious that every mile they could put between themselves and the Marauders was time well spent. Apart from water, he felt that time was the most precious commodity in the world for him and Beth Lassiter.

Beth struggled to gain wakefulness, and was initially confused by the gentle swaying back and forth as she sat on the burro. She rubbed her eyes and saw the tall figure of Jake Scudder walking ahead of the animal, leading it by its reins.

'Jake, you must be exhausted,' she said.

He turned and flashed a smile at her. 'Morning, Beth. And exhausted just about sums it up, but we've got to keep going. I'm guessing that those Marauders will be coming after us any time now.'

'Have we come far?'

'Far enough to give us a chance.'

'You mentioned Todd Brodie, the train driver, last night. Will he be OK?'

Jake gave a wan smile and unconsciously felt for his jaw, which still ached from a punch that Todd had landed on him. He nodded. 'I reckon wherever he is he'll be doing just fine, Beth. He's a tough dude.'

Even in the pale light of early morning he noticed the way she gave a half smile and nodded her head as if fondly picturing the railroad driver.

'Excuse me for asking, Beth, but do you know Todd?'

She shook her head. 'No, I . . . I have barely spoken to him. I just . . . we just . . . noticed each other.'

Jake gave a short laugh. 'The ways of the world are strange, Beth. Take Ruby-May Prescott and me, we barely met and yet I can hardly get her out of my mind.' He laughed again. 'The thing is, I do believe that she felt the same way about me.'

'Then I truly hope that we can get out of this mess,' Beth said. 'Where should we try to get to? Back to Coopersville?'

Jake shook his head. 'I can't risk going there, Beth.'

'But surely if you are with me you will be safe. And knowing all that I know we can persuade people that — '

'I reckon some hothead would just as likely shoot me on sight.' He stopped and ran a hand over the burro's crown. 'I figure that there is only one place that we can go. We've got to go to the Curly P ranch.'

'To Uncle Hank's!' Beth gasped. 'I . . . I never thought I'd see the place again, but I expect you're right.'

Jake rubbed his eyes and Beth realized how tired he must be. 'We'll have to go past Clem Brookes's place first and maybe see if we can pick up another burro; that is as long as no one has taken the poor critter away.' He yawned and added, 'Some shut-eye wouldn't go amiss. My brain's starting to get a bit muddled.'

★ ★ ★

Sheriff Dan Foster was aware that he was well nigh facing a mutiny. After the noise of the explosions the night before he had made the posse hunker down and wait for daybreak. No fires, no comforts like coffee or smokes, just quiet and wakefulness to try to catch the sound of movement anywhere. His hope was that if anyone was on the move their best chance of catching them was by stealth, the way a trapdoor spider would wait and pounce out to catch its prey.

But by daybreak they had heard nothing. Now the men were all for abandoning the search.

'I got a family to feed.'

'And my belly needs feeding too, Sheriff.'

'Damned fool's errand this has been.'

The sheriff scowled, and then nodded

his head. 'OK, OK, I agree, we'll head back to Coopersville. Let's fill up with a coffee first.'

And several miles away Baxter Walsh was having a similar argument with Zach Harding.

'Why do I think you've been making us circle round and round these canyons? We should have tracked these crooks by now — especially when they'd set off those damned explosions to lead us to them.

The rancher squared up to the railroad boss. 'We don't know it was the outlaws. These mountains are full of old prospectors who live half their lives underground in two-bit mines.'

'Yeah, and they go blasting in the middle of the night,' Walsh replied sarcastically. 'How do I know you aren't in league with these Marauders?'

'I'd be careful if I was you, Walsh!' Zach Harding grated.

'Like you've been careful with this posse? Where's poor old Norton? He could be dead for all I know.'

'Norton's your man, isn't he?' He prodded the railroad boss with a finger. 'It's you that needs to be careful if you ask me. Now saddle up and back off.'

Baxter Walsh's mouth curved into a smile that lacked humour. 'You want me to back off, do you? Maybe you'd like me to disappear.' He half turned, then suddenly spun round and gave the rancher a crack on the jaw.

Instantly guns were drawn from holsters and weapons aimed at Walsh. But Zach Harding stayed them with a raised hand. 'Easy boys. Mr Walsh here is just upset,' he said, rubbing his jaw and again squaring up to Walsh. 'I'm going to let that pass for now. But when we get back to Coopersville, I reckon I'm going to want satisfaction, man to man.'

'Any way you want it, cowboy!' returned the railroad boss, stomping off towards his horse.

★ ★ ★

The Marauders were also up and off at daybreak. Before they left, Frank Griggs once again had words with Norton.

'We found Manson, like I thought we would. And we've found the dead horse and the direction they went in. One man and a woman. That Scudder has sealed his own death warrant. I reckon we ought to catch up with them in an hour or two, and then I'm going to settle with him once and for all.'

'And the woman?'

Griggs nodded. 'And the woman.' He lit a quirly. 'You just sit tight and when we get back we'll do what we need to.' The outlaw leader took a deep draw on his quirly and picked a loose strand of tobacco from his lip. 'And while we're gone I've got a little job for you. You can plant Tallisker, Manson and Grover afore the buzzards decide to hone in for breakfast and lead the posse to us. Oh yeah — and the horse, too.'

Norton reverted to butler mode and bobbed his head. 'Consider it taken care of.'

He stood sipping his mug of coffee as he watched the Marauders ride out. He knew that Frank Griggs was a vicious killer, and that his threat of the night before would be no idle one. But he was under no illusions about himself. He had hardly lived the life of a saint. He had been forced to leave England in a hurry to save his neck from the gallows. Once in America he had capitalized on his accent and managed to get work as a butler on the strength of it. It was easy enough work, if you didn't mind a bit of forelock tugging and being lorded over.

The thing was that Norton had limits of endurance, then, when they were reached, he was liable to snap. And that was just what had happened when a swanky New York lawyer who had employed him on a trial basis went too far with the lording business. By the time they found his body, with his throat neatly cut from ear to ear, Norton had vanished westwards.

He took a final swig of coffee and

savoured it, just as he savoured the thought of dispatching Frank Griggs in the same way. Quietly and neatly in the dead of the night with a blade. He tossed the dregs of the coffee onto the ground then returned to the cabin to inspect the pile of strongboxes.

'Those bird-bait corpses can wait awhile,' he mused to himself. 'First I've got to work out a way of getting the gold out of these boxes without making any noise. Can't risk any explosions.' He knelt down by them and stroked his stubbly chin. 'How come Griggs hasn't even tried opening them? It doesn't make much sense!'

He was puzzling the matter over when he became aware of a shadow that had suddenly fallen across the strongboxes. He turned slowly, and squinted at the shape of a man standing in the sunlit doorway. Then he smiled as he recognized the newcomer.

'Well thank the lord! If it isn't my good friend Todd Brodie.' He stood up and held out his hand, only to stop when he saw the old Peacemaker in the train driver's hand.

His expression became pained. 'What's the gun for, Todd? You know me. Sidney Norton — Mr Walsh's butler.' He pointed to the pile of strongboxes. 'You don't think I had anything to do with all this, do you?' Then his expression changed again, to one of joy. 'I can't tell you how pleased I am to see you still alive. I thought you'd died in that crash, like all — '

'Like Chuck and Willie,' Todd volunteered. 'Or that deputy sheriff, Luke Curren?'

Norton made the sign of a cross and clicked his tongue. 'It was a great tragedy. And those Marauders, they kidnapped Miss Lassiter. I trailed them here.'

'And where have they gone now, Sidney?' Todd asked, with as much affability as he could manage.

'They've gone off someplace. That Jake Scudder, the murderer, he's taken the girl. I was hiding and watching

185

them, trying to find a moment to try to rescue the girl. There just wasn't a chance, Todd.'

He had taken a small step towards the driver. He nodded at the gun still levelled at him. 'You're making me feel a tad nervous with that cannon of yours.' He grinned, then: 'How about you put it away?'

In response Todd pulled back the hammer and Norton stood stock still, his eyes widening in alarm. 'I don't think so,' Todd snapped. 'Put your hands up, Norton.'

The butler slowly raised his hands. 'What's this about, Todd?'

'You are a snivelling, murdering liar, Norton — and I wouldn't trust you as far as I could throw you.'

Norton looked pained. 'But I'm your friend, Todd. We both work for Mr Walsh. For the SWC Railroad.'

'I've been following you ever since the loco crash. I was there when you got the message about doing away with Beth Lassiter.' He looked disgustedly at the butler. 'And I was watching when you broke that outlaw's neck as if you were wringing a chicken's neck.'

Norton said nothing for a moment, then inexplicably he grinned. 'Well, I suppose there's no point in trying to spin a tale any more, is there Todd?'

'None at all, you low life.'

Norton gestured behind him with a nod of the head. 'Come on, mate,' he cooed, 'why don't you and me work together? There's a fortune in those chests. We could split it fifty-fifty and be out of here before they all come back.'

'So you'd rob the rest of your gang as well.'

'It's a fortune, mate. You could buy your own railroad if you wanted.'

'You're going to hang, do you know that? Just like you and the rest of your Marauder scum planned to let Jake Scudder hang.'

'That was none of my doing.'

Todd gestured with his gun. 'With your left hand slowly undo your gunbelt and let it drop to the floor. Then kick it towards me.'

The butler gingerly did as he was bid. 'Are you going to shoot me, Todd?'

'I ought to. But you deserve to hang.'

Norton smiled smugly and shook his head. 'Do you think that you can make me come back with you? You'd never get past the Marauders.'

Todd pointed to the gaping hole in the side of the cabin. 'The Marauders aren't so tough, I reckon. Jake Scudder has the girl all right, I overheard everything and I know that the rest of the gang are chasing them right now.'

'You do, do you? Then how comes you didn't sidle off yourself in the middle of the night instead of waiting to get caught by the Marauders when they come back? Seems to me you're just a stupid big oaf of a railroad driver.'

It was Todd's turn to smile. 'Actually, I waited until they'd gone because I wanted to get you alone.'

Norton sneered. 'Well, I don't reckon you've got the guts to take me in. And I doubt if you even know how to fire that cannon.'

Todd hefted the big revolver and shrugged. 'You may be right. Maybe this thing could just go off and blow you away.'

'Yeah, and bring the rest of the gang back here pronto. I think I won't come with you after all.'

He made to step towards his discarded gunbelt, but the icy tone in Todd's voice halted him.

'Move a muscle towards that gun and I will take the greatest of pleasure in blowing your brains out. Even a dumb railroad driver like me couldn't miss at this range.' He took a couple of steps backwards and gestured with the Peacemaker in his fist. 'Step out here into the open, mister.'

Norton complied, then stood staring in amazement as Todd uncocked the gun and let it drop from his grasp.

'I'm going to give you a chance, Norton. Not that you deserve it.'

A thin smile played across the

butler's mouth. 'You want me to fight you?'

Todd raised his fists. 'Man to man. I'm going to enjoy beating you to a pulp. For Willie and Chuck.'

'You really are stupid, aren't you, Todd,' Norton scoffed, reaching behind him and suddenly drawing out a derringer from his waistband. 'This is a gentleman's weapon,' he said. 'I'm sorry but I must decline your offer of a fist fight. So it's goodbye.'

He pulled back the twin hammers of the derringer.

Todd's shoulders had seemed to slump and Norton tossed his head back and laughed, revelling in the ease with which he had managed to fool the big man. He was still laughing as he saw a blur of movement as Todd grabbed the axe that had been tucked into the back of his trousers and in one swift movement tossed it at the butler. It spun a couple of times on its way and embedded itself with a sickening thump in Norton's throat.

The renegade butler fell back on the ground, his eyes staring in horror as blood spurted from his wound and a gurgling noise came from his throat.

'I figured you'd try something like that,' said Todd dispassionately, as he looked down at the writhing Norton. 'I'm afraid I'm not a gentleman like you. I'm just a dumb railroad driver, hence this crude weapon of mine.'

He reached down, grabbed the handle of the axe, then with a foot on the side of the butler's blood-spurting neck he yanked it free. Another jet of blood gushed out and Norton made futile attempts to close the wound in his throat and to speak. His eyes fixed Todd pleadingly.

Todd squatted down beside the dying man. 'I heard that Griggs feller tell you to bury the horse and those three dead bodies. He didn't want the vultures to lead the posse here.' He looked up at the cobalt blue sky where a couple of unmistakable shapes were circling high overhead. 'The thing is, Norton —

mate, as you say — I have no such worries.'

Norton stared in terror, his life blood slowly seeping away.

'Besides, I've had enough grave-digging,' Todd said, straightening up. 'So long, Norton.'

10

It was mid-morning by the time Jake and Beth eventually made their way down the rocky trail out of the Pintos towards Clem Brookes's place. Once they arrived Jake loosed Shifty into the corral where the other burro trotted over to greet him.

'I wish I could leave you here for a good long rest,' Jake said to the animal as he watched it lap up a second bucketful of water, instantly re-hydrating itself as these creatures of the semi-desert regions were able to do. 'The thing is that we're going to have to move along soon and take your friend here with us.'

A quick search in a small shed tacked on to the rear of the cabin yielded a couple of ancient saddles and a saddle-bag. He hoisted them out and immediately began saddling the two burros up.

Beth appeared from the cabin carrying a canteen and a small parcel. 'It's hardly home cooking, but I found a few crusts and some salted pork belly,' she said, crossing the yard. She pointed to the freshly dug mound of earth by the side of the cabin. 'Is that — ?'

'Yeah, that's old Clem Brookes's grave. Todd and I laid him to rest and had a makeshift prayer over him.'

Beth handed him the parcel and he stuffed it inside the saddle-bag. 'Don't you think we have time for a coffee?'

Jake hung the canteen from the pommel of his saddle and shook his head emphatically. 'We've got to move as fast as we can, Beth. The Marauders could be on us any time now. We've got to put some distance between us.' He patted Shifty. 'These burros are great in the mountains, but on open trails they can't match a horse for speed. Come on now, let's get you to safety at Hank's place.'

Beth accepted his assistance to mount

her new burro. 'I can't say that I'm looking forward to seeing his place. Not now that he'll never be coming back.'

Jake put a hand on her shoulder and squeezed. 'I know, it's tough, Beth. But for now it's the safest place we can go.' His stomach rumbled and he patted the saddle-bag.

'Are you OK eating as we ride? My stomach's feeling awful close to my backbone and even this old leather saddlebag is looking good enough to eat.'

For the first time in days Beth found herself laughing. It broke the tension and they both found themselves laughing as they headed out of the old linesman's corral. But the laughter did not last long, for they knew that men were chasing them and that they had death planned for them.

* * *

Dan Foster was leading his posse in single file along the bottom of the sheer-faced ravines that characterized the Pintos. Despite himself, the hairs on the back of his neck were standing up, for it was, he felt, a dandy place for an ambush. He was relieved, therefore, when the trail finally opened out to allow several of the other riders to come alongside him.

'What you planning to do next, Dan?' asked Jubal Jones, the Coopersville liveryman. 'Are you going to call in the army for help?'

Sheriff Foster shook his head. 'The army won't be interested in a local matter like this, Jubal. It would be a different matter if an army pay-roll had been stolen, but this was bank money and a civilian kidnapping.' He shook his head. 'No, I reckon I might have to wire the US marshal, or maybe team up with Sheriff Olafson at Logan City and take a fresh posse out here.'

'I reckon you'd be wasting your time,' interjected a rangy cowboy called Elmer Bell, who had come with the town posse when they had split from the others. 'There isn't any way you'll find those Marauders in the Pintos. You could lose a whole army in here.' He spat a stream of tobacco juice at a nearby cactus. 'Even old Hannibal and all his elephants could just disappear in here.'

And he and Jubal Jones began to laugh.

Then Sheriff Foster silenced them by suddenly raising his arm.

'What's the matter, Sheriff? You think — ?'

Dan Foster cut him off with a steely look, then closed his eyes as if trying hard to concentrate on something.

'I heard something,' he said softly, as the rest of the posse stopped behind them, muttering among themselves. 'It was horses.'

His hand went to his side and he patted the handle of his Peacemaker. 'All of you get ready, boys,' he said, turning in the saddle. 'We may be in for some action after all.'

Baxter Walsh was smarting. He was not used to being an outsider. Normally he was the man that people listened to, who folk fawned over and went to lengths to impress. But not so any of this group of men, all of whom seemed loyal to Zach Harding, the man he had confronted a few hours earlier and actually struck out at — who inexplicably hadn't reacted as he would have done. And bizarrely, to Walsh's mind, it had put them all staunchly behind the rancher and against him.

And he wondered where the hell his butler, Norton, had gone to. In a way he felt responsible for him. He had visions of the man, used to waiting on others, just getting more and more lost in the maze of canyons and ravines that made up the Pintos.

He was rudely awakened from his pensive reverie by Zach Harding himself, who had suddenly dropped back to ride beside him.

'We'll be back in Coopersville in a few hours, Walsh,' he announced coldly. 'Then you and I are going to sort out our differences.' He stared the railroad boss squarely in the eyes. 'Unless you want to apologize to me — in front of all my men.'

Baxter Walsh had made his fortune by being positive, by gambling here and there, but always taking a firm stance when he felt he was right. And he felt that he had right on his side at the moment.

'In that case, I apologize if I hurt your feelings — but I am not sorry for the punch. You deserved it!'

Zach Harding glared at him. 'Then you had better start praying, because I'm going to take you up on your word. We'll sort this out like gentlemen — with guns!'

Baxter Walsh's heart either missed a beat or pumped an extra one, he wasn't exactly sure which, but his face didn't register any emotion at all. His business acumen and his poker ability had long since taught him that if you wanted to win then you had to give your opponent no clue about what you were feeling or thinking.

'Guns it is then,' he replied simply.

And a split-second later he found himself reaching for his own Colt .45 when he saw Zach Harding go for the Remington at his side.

'Don't be a fool!' hissed Harding. 'I'm not drawing on you. I thought I heard something.'

The rest of the posse had already stopped and were looking back at the rancher and the railroad boss.

'I hear horses — nearby!' Zach Harding said urgently.

★   ★   ★

The Curly P ranch was far lusher in comparison to the Lazy H range that bound it on one side, and the craggy rocks and stacks that abutted it on the other.

'Looks like your uncle was right

about the water on this spread,' Jake remarked to Beth. 'It looks to be the best range for miles around here.'

'But there's no livestock,' Beth replied. 'It looks eerie — like a ghost ranch.' And despite the heat of the day, she shivered.

'I guess they took all of the hogs back to Coopersville,' Jake said, indicating a series of empty adobe walled pens. 'They've probably already made arrangements to ship them out for slaughter.'

Beth pursed her lips. 'If only I could have seen him one last time. I owed him so much. He paid for all of my education. And we had such plans.'

'And that's the reason you were coming out here?

Beth nodded. 'I was going to start a school.'

'That's just what every growing community needs,' Jake replied. 'Education is the real frontier-blazer.'

He pointed to the surprisingly well-maintained ranch house ahead. It was a single-storied building with a long porch, a pair of chimneys and a large window that took up half of the right side of the building.

The sun glinted on the glass and Jake had a momentary impression that there was someone inside, watching them.

'Hold up a moment, Beth,' he said, reaching for and grasping the reins on her burro. 'I think there is — '

And in that moment the front door of the ranch house was thrown open and a woman's figure appeared.

'Jake! I thought you might come here!' cried Ruby-May Prescott as she jumped down from the porch and ran to meet him.

Jake threw a leg over the burro and met her at a run.

'Ruby-May!' he cried. 'I swear — '

He collected her in his arms as her arms snaked around his neck and she silenced him with a kiss.

Beth, embarrassed for a moment, rode past them then dismounted in front of the ranch house. As she was tying the reins of her burro on to a hitching post with a carved pig on top she gasped as a thin figure limped out of the doorway, a gun in his hand.

'That's enough! Stop right there, Jake Scudder, and raise your hands in the air,' Judge Leroy Anderson barked.

The noise of the hammer of a Colt .45 being ratcheted back was unmistakeable. 'Or so help me, I will drop you right where you stand. Step away from him, Ruby-May.'

Ruby-May Prescott refused to move and kept her arms about him. Instead, she swivelled round so that her own body was between Jake and the judge.

'You just stop that, Leroy Anderson!' she said forcefully. 'What the hell are you playing at — after all we talked about.'

'This man is a convicted murderer, Ruby-May,' the judge persisted. 'And he's going to die — either by the rope or the bullet, so God is my witness.'

'Then you'll have to shoot me too, Judge,' Ruby-May cried back. Jake could feel her bosom heaving against his chest. Then she added: 'Holster that gun, Judge, and let's all go inside and talk. Or haven't you noticed that he's got Beth Lassiter with him?'

Judge Anderson's brow furrowed and he looked uncertain, a state that was usually foreign to him.

Beth took three paces and touched his arm. 'She's right, Judge. Jake Scudder never murdered anyone. I know that. Now let's go inside and talk.'

The judge hesitated for a moment, then: 'OK, but I'm keeping this gun ready. And I want Scudder to shuck all of that weaponry and Ruby-May you carry it inside.'

Jake did as he was bidden. He unbuckled his gunbelt and handed it to Ruby-May. Then he leaned forward and gently kissed her, before walking towards the ranch house. 'All I want is a fair hearing, Judge,' he said.

'You already had that, mister,' the judge returned acerbically. 'Whatever you say had better be extra good. I'm not the sort of judge who doubts his own judgements, you just remember that.'

Once inside the ranch house the judge pointed to a chair beside the large window. 'Sit where I can see you, Scudder,' he ordered. Then turning, his tone changing: 'Take a seat ladies.'

Beth sat on a battered swivel-chair beside an open roll-top desk, while Ruby-May sat down on a worn armchair underneath a painting of two young men wearing the uniform of the confederacy. Their resemblance to Beth was unmistakeable and Jake correctly concluded that one was a youthful Hank Lassiter and the other his brother, Beth's father. Ruby-May looped the gun-belt over the arm of the chair.

'All right, mister, tell me your story,' the judge snapped.

And Jake did just that. He recounted his tale from first meeting and rescuing Hank Lassiter until the locomotive crash at Horse Neck Bridge.

'And then the Marauders kidnapped

me,' Beth continued. 'And that awful man, Norton, Baxter Walsh's so-called butler was a member of the gang.'

'But they had no intention of just holding Beth for ransom,' Jake pointed out.

And between them they recounted Beth's ordeal and her rescue from the Marauders' hideout.

Ruby-May let out a little shriek of indignation. 'Those vermin! They were going to rape you?'

Beth nodded. She smiled at Jake. 'They would have if it hadn't been for Mr Scudder here. Suddenly she coloured. 'And Mr Brodie, the locomotive driver, is still in the Pintos somewhere. I hope he's — '

'Todd Brodie will be just fine, Beth,' Jake reassured her. 'That man is one heck of a survivor.'

Judge Leroy Anderson had been standing all this time with his gun covering Jake. He was clearly uncomfortable and beginning to fidget, as if his leg was causing him some pain. He took a couple of backward paces and sat on the edge of Hank Lassiter's table. 'This is all very well,' he said at last, 'and I don't doubt that there has been some double-dealing going on — but none of this alters my original judgement. You haven't given me one single bit of evidence to show that you didn't kill Hank Lassiter.'

Ruby-May sighed in exasperation. 'Dammit, Leroy Anderson, haven't you heard a thing? Use your brain. Of course Jake didn't kill Hank Lassiter. It was someone from the Marauders.'

Jake nodded. 'My guess is that it was those two varmints who tried to bushwack Hank and me — Manson and Grover, were their names.'

Beth shivered. 'Grover was the one who tried to rape me.'

The judge pursed his lips then peered past Jake, his eyes screwing up to look through the window. 'Now who the hell is this?' he queried. 'By the size of that dust cloud it looks like a sizeable number of riders.'

'I guess it will be Frank Griggs and his Marauders,' Jake speculated. 'And their plan is to kill Beth and me.'

'That's rubbish!' exclaimed the judge. But his troubled expression belied his words. He knew only too well that if it was Frank Griggs then his own life was at serious risk.

He turned to the saloon owner. 'Ruby-May, what do you think — ?'

There was the deafening report of a Colt .45 and Judge Leroy Anderson's body was suddenly jolted. He looked down at his chest, where a rapidly expanding patch of red was spreading out from an ugly bullet wound over his heart. Then he looked up at Ruby-May, who was standing with a smoking gun held firmly in her outstretched hand.

'I think it's time for you to die — you evil old lecher!' she said between gritted teeth.

Beth screamed as the judge mouthed the word 'why,' then pitched forward, dead without knowing why he had been killed.

Jake had started to his feet despite his shock, but Ruby-May immediately trained the gun on him.

'Ruby-May, why the hell — ?' he demanded.

Beth had slowly risen to her feet. 'It's just become clear to me. You knew we'd come here, didn't you?'

Ruby-May's lips curved into a feline smile. 'Woman's intuition,' she replied. 'If you managed to escape I figured it would be the only place you would think was safe. And I must admit I was surprised when you did show up. But I still had to go along with my little charade, for the judge's sake.'

Beth looked distastefully at the saloon owner. 'You are the real boss of the Marauders, aren't you?'

Ruby-May nodded. 'And soon I'm going to be the richest woman in the whole territory, what with the bank's money, this valuable little ranch, which you are about to sign over to me, and the SWC Railroad and maybe a couple more ranches that I'm going to pick up.' She grinned maliciously and added, 'One way or the other. I have Walsh and Harding eating out of my hand. I guess one of them will kill the other sometime, and then I'll take the other one, until a little accident — '

'You'll never have this ranch,' Beth said defiantly. 'Not as long as I live.'

'Which may not be long, my dear.'

Jake shook his head in disbelief. 'You sure had me fooled, Ruby-May. I thought that we — '

'That we what? Had something going?' she sneered. 'You men are all such fools. I needed to make sure that Hank Lassiter didn't sell his land to either Zach Harding or Baxter Walsh. The last thing I wanted was for a railroad to cut through to the south. Coopersville would just become a ghost town if we were by-passed. We had already taken care of the banker and had the bank money in the bag ready for the taking.'

'So the locomotive crash was all pre-arranged?' Jake gasped.

'In principle. It was just a matter of timing. And then you came along and gave us a good opportunity to get rid of Hank Lassiter once and for all.' She beamed. 'And now I'm not even going to have to buy this ranch. You're going to give it to me.'

'So you're going to kill us both?' Beth asked, her voice trembling.

Ruby-May pointed out of the window and laughed. 'Not me, my dear. The boys will oblige!'

The Marauders were fast approaching.

11

Jake Scudder stared at the woman that he thought he had fallen in love with and slowly shook his head. From the corner of his eye, through the window, he could see the dust cloud and blur of movement that heralded the imminent arrival of the Marauders — and certain death for him and Beth.

'In that case, Ruby-May,' he said with a wan smile. 'I guess you're going to have to murder us as well as the judge.' And he took a step towards her.

Ruby-May's eyes opened wider. She had not expected this. Her lips curled into an unattractive snarl. 'You asked for it, big man!' And raising the gun directly at his chest she pulled the trigger.

The hammer fell home with a metallic click, but there was no explosion, no recoil. Then with both hands she desperately pulled back the hammer.

But it was too late. In two more quick paces Jake had reached her and grabbed the barrel of the gun, wrenching it from her grasp. The gun went off and a bullet embedded itself in the painting of the Lassiter brothers, between their heads.

'I never thought I'd ever hit a woman,' Jake said, chopping down on the side of the saloon owner's head with the butt of the gun. 'But you are one evil witch!'

Beth gasped as Ruby-May fell to the ground. 'Jake, she could have shot you! How did you dare — ?'

Jake swiftly bound Ruby-May's wrists with his bandanna. He looked up at Beth Lassiter with a whimsical grin on his face. 'It's an old habit of mine. I put a dollar bill in one of the chambers of the gun when I reloaded. I knew it was either the second or the third round. I knew I had a sort of chance.'

His face hardened. 'Now you just

stay out of the line of this window, Beth.' And so saying he hauled Ruby-May along the floor until he was under the window, then he cautiously peered over the ledge. 'We're still in a tight spot here. The Marauders will be on us in a minute at the most.' He indicated his gunbelt and the judge's gun that lay by his face-down body. 'Slide those across to me then go and have a look out of the back. I guess you'll find Ruby-May's horse and the judge's.'

Beth did as she was bidden and returned a moment later. 'You were right, they're out there and all saddled. Are we going to try to make a run for it, Jake?'

Jake had taken the opportunity to reload his gun and check the judge's weapon. He shook his head. 'It was just an idea. But I think we're going to be too late. They're here.'

He gave her a reassuring smile that she didn't think he really meant, then: 'Desperate measures call for desperate action,' he mused. He reached over and dragged the swivel-chair towards him. He hefted it for a moment, and then flung it over his head, smashing the large window.

Frank Griggs and the Marauders were a mere thirty yards from the ranch house. They reined up as soon as they saw the chair smash through the window.

'Back off, Griggs!' Jake cried. 'Unless you want to taste some lead.'

Frank Griggs casually unholstered his gun. He tossed his head back and laughed. 'Well, well, Scudder. So you reckon you're going to fight us all off by yourself. You're a dead man. A condemned man. Maybe the boys here will just come in and save the law a job. I reckon we can find some old tree to string you up.' His lips tightened. 'Now come on out and bring the woman with you.'

'You all just stay where you are,' Jake cried. 'I'm going to show you a woman, all right.'

He put an arm round Ruby-May's waist and lifted her as easily as if she had been a doll. He rose with her in front of him, the barrel of his Colt .45 at her temple, which was already blue and swollen.

'The question is — which woman!' he cried. 'I've got your boss here, Griggs. And I know all about your plans.'

Frank Griggs was unused to surprises and he cursed. 'Nobody fire,' he hissed to his men. Then he nodded to the two Marauders on each flank. 'When I drop my hand you two make for the back of the house. We'll surround the bastard.'

He raised his hand in a sign of peace. 'OK, Scudder. Let's talk. What do you want?'

'You all to ride off the way you came — or die right here.'

Griggs shook his head. 'Brave talk, Scudder, but I'm afraid I can't oblige.' He dropped his hand and immediately the Marauder called Red and a swarthy hatless rider set off to circle the ranch house.

Jake had expected such a move and his gun belched flame twice in rapid succession and both outlaws fell from their saddles. A third shot spun the outlaw immediately to Frank Griggs's left backwards out of his saddle with a bullet through the head.

'Take cover!' Griggs said, dismounting in a single move and diving for the protection of a couple of barrels. The others followed suit and took up what cover they could behind adobe pig-pens, feeding troughs and stacks of wood.

Ruby-May had come back to consciousness and stared in horror at the scene in front of her, and at her bound wrists. 'Frank! Be careful — ' she yelled urgently.

But she was silenced as Jake ducked down, dragging her with him and depositing her unceremoniously on the floor.

'Scudder, you hurt a hair on her head and I'll take a pleasure in killing you real slow.'

A couple of the Marauders had drawn

their weapons and let off a couple of shots at the window, showering the trio inside with shards of glass.

'Don't shoot, damn you!' Griggs snarled at them. 'Don't do anything unless I tell you.'

'That's right, boys,' Jake called, peeping out of the window. 'But maybe you'd all better take a look behind you.'

Frank Griggs cast a rapid eye over his shoulder and cursed the fact that they had let their horses run off. He had not anticipated any problem in them being able to round them up as soon as they dealt with Scudder. But the cloud of dust that heralded another group of riders coming up the trail at speed was unexpected to say the least. Almost immediately beads of perspiration began to form on his brow. All of the Marauders were suddenly exposed to an attack from behind. Things seemed to be going wrong all of a sudden.

★ ★ ★

Dan Foster cried to his posse to dismount and trail-hitch their horses by the far hog-pen walls.

'Now we're going to get them, boys,' he said, propping his Winchester atop the wall and taking aim. 'Let them have it!'

Jubal Jones looked doubtfully at the sheriff for a moment. 'Ain't we going to give them a chance to surrender, and then arrest them?'

Dan Foster let off a shot and immediately one of the Marauders slumped against the pen wall he was hiding behind. 'Nope! These men are vermin. You've all seen what they've done. We're going to give them no quarter.'

One of the posse smirked. 'It'll be like shooting fish in a barrel!' And he took aim and another Marauder fell dead, as the rest of the gang began to return fire.

'Hell, Frank,' one of the Marauders cried, 'we've got to get into that ranch house afore they pick us off like crows.'

He vaulted the stack of wood he had positioned himself behind and immediately winced as a bullet tore into his right arm and he dropped his weapon.

'If anybody else has the idea of taking shelter this way then they either throw their guns this way first, or expect me to do more permanent damage to them,' Jake called out. 'And if you do come you just stay put there, because I've got a gun on you.'

As the posse continued its barrage and three more Marauders were hit, two fatally and one cripplingly, four of the others threw their guns towards the ranch house and jumped over their shelters for protection, where they remained as petrified as rabbits hemmed in by a parcel of rattlers.

Frank Griggs, who had dived behind a couple of barrels, had managed to haul one round, thereby giving him a measure of protection in both directions. He raised his hat and called out, 'That you, Sheriff Foster? Reckon we've got a bit of a stand-off here. I reckon we need to parley.'

'Why's that, Griggs?' Foster returned.

'Because we've got Scudder pinned in here, and he's holding that Lassiter woman and Ruby-May Prescott.'

Sheriff Foster raised his hand. 'Hold your fire men,' he said, pensively. 'Looks like we've got ourselves a situation here.'

In the ranch house Jake looked round at Ruby-May who was lying on the floor, half propped up against the desk. 'Seems they all think you're actually worth something,' he said distastefully.

'You don't know the half of it,' she returned contemptuously. 'Either one of them will save me — and kill you!' She looked hatefully at Beth Lassiter and added, 'Both of you!'

★ ★ ★

Jubal Jones the livery man had felt uneasy about the way Sheriff Foster had unleashed lead on the Marauders without first offering to let them surrender. He turned at the sound of horses coming from behind them. The noise of their gunfire had muffled their approach.

'Looks like the rest of the posse has found us, Sheriff. Now we've got too many men for them to argue about, I reckon.'

And moments later they were joined by Baxter Walsh, Zach Harding and the others.

Sheriff Foster quickly outlined the problem as they all took up protective positions as best they could. Then he raised his voice: 'Jake Scudder! This is Sheriff Foster. You are under arrest. I want you to come out of that ranch house with your hands above your head. I guarantee safe passage.'

'Hold on there, Sheriff,' said Baxter Walsh. 'Jake Scudder is an innocent man. We know it, don't we, Harding?'

The rancher nodded. 'Todd Brodie the loco driver told us all about it. Griggs and his Marauders have been working in league with someone in town.'

'You're crazy,' returned the sheriff in disbelief.

Then they heard Beth Lassiter's voice. 'Judge Anderson's body is here,' she announced, shouting over Jake's shoulder. 'Ruby-May Prescott shot him in front of us. She's the boss of the Marauders.'

Between his barrels, Frank Griggs tossed his head back and laughed. 'You OK in there, Ruby-May?' he called. 'Sounds like it is all over. So why don't you ask Scudder and Miss Lassiter to bring you out to see the good sheriff?'

Ruby-May's face contorted with rage. 'You're a fool and a liar, Frank Griggs. You're going to die.' And then raising her voice even louder: 'Sheriff Foster, you've got to save me.'

Griggs snorted. 'That's right, Danny boy. You gotta rescue her. And while you're at it you better let me and my boys go.'

Dan Foster bit his lip. He whispered to the members of the posse, 'We can't trust either of them. We'll rush them when I say now — '

He was interrupted by Todd Brodie's urgent interjection. He had been relieved to hear Beth Lassiter's voice, but her words had brought the memory of the other night back to him with crystal clarity.

'It's you!' he said accusingly, pointing his finger at the sheriff. 'You were the one talking to Norton that night in the Pintos. I recognize your voice. She's your boss too! You're in it with them.'

'You're a liar and a fool!' replied the sheriff, his face suddenly pale.

★ ★ ★

Beth Lassiter suddenly felt her hair tugged backwards, forcing her throat upwards — and she felt the long shard of glass cut into her skin.

'Drop those guns now!' Ruby-May snapped at Jake. 'And then turn round really slowly, or I'll slice her throat open.'

Jake immediately did as he was told and turned to see Beth's petrified face, an ugly long sliver of glass held to her throat by the saloon owner, Ruby-May Prescott.

'Thanks for giving me the means of cutting myself free,' she said. 'Now slide those guns across the floor towards that back door.'

And as Jake complied, Ruby-May half dragged Beth with her. Then at the door she flung her inwards, picked up the guns and ran for the back door. But not before she cried, 'Get ready, Frank!'

* * *

Before any of the posse could say anything Sheriff Foster raised his gun at Todd and fired. Then, as they all watched in horror as Todd spun backwards, he grabbed Zach Harding about the neck and put his gun to his temple.

'All of you just let your weapons drop to the ground,' he barked. 'All of you! That is if you want this cowboy fool to live!'

The Lazy H crew seemed to hesitate, then as if of one accord they dropped their hardware and watched impotently as the town sheriff frog-marched the popular rancher backwards towards the trail-hitched horses.

'If anyone — and I mean anyone — moves, I'll blow his head off.'

Baxter Walsh had not complied. He raised his weapon and took a pace after the sheriff and his prisoner. 'What makes you think I'd worry about that, Sheriff?' he asked. 'Harding and I aren't exactly friends. Go ahead. Shoot him. Then try me.'

* * *

One of the Marauders whispered urgently to Frank Griggs, terror in his voice. 'What the hell we are we going to do now, Frank? You got any ideas?'

The cadence of galloping horses came from the side of the ranch house and a moment later Ruby-May Prescott appeared riding a bay and leading a pinto by its reins.

'Not sure about you boys,' Griggs said with a grin, striking a match against the side of the barrel and applying it to the fuse of a stick of dynamite. 'But me, I always like to be prepared. I'm going to blast my way out.'

And rising to his feet he hurled the dynamite towards the posse, then running towards the galloping horses he caught the pommel of the pinto's saddle and vaulted. His foot landed in the stirrup and he hauled himself up.

'Good girl,' he shouted with a grin. 'Pity about the double-cross you planned!' And drawing his gun he shot her in the chest and she fell sideways to be dragged bumping up and down by her boot that remained stuck in its stirrup.

'Dynamite!' Jubal Jones had cried upon seeing the sizzling stick arc through the air, simultaneous with the noise of horses. It hit the ground nearby and all of their attention was focused on it and self-preservation. The noise of a gun-shot didn't even register as they tried to take what cover they could.

Except for the sheriff, his prisoner, Zach Harding, and Baxter Walsh, all of whom seemed frozen out, in a sort of world of their own. Sheriff Dan Foster had been in many a tight corner, but none as tight as this one. He hesitated for a moment, then began to swivel his gun towards the railroad boss. But it was a moment too long.

Baxter Walsh fired. Zach Harding felt a searing pain as the top of his left ear was torn away and he was dragged backwards. It took a moment for him to realize that he was still alive. Then he was being dragged upwards, off Sheriff Dan Foster whose faceless body was beginning to convulse in a final death-throe.

'Come on — move!' barked Baxter Walsh, half dragging, half throwing the rancher over the low wall of a hog-pen.

They just cleared it before the dynamite exploded a few yards away.

★ ★ ★

As the fireball cleared to be replaced by a pall of smoke and falling debris, Jake flung himself through the shattered window and rolled a couple of times as he attempted to reach the guns that some of the Marauders had tossed towards the ranch house. He reached them just before two of the gang. He pistol-whipped one and took the other out with a straight left to the jaw.

Frank Griggs was viciously spurring the pinto on and disappeared into the pall of smoke adding to the confusion.

Jake ran, spying Shifty, the burro that he had grown so attached to, standing drinking at a trough despite all of the

229

noise that had gone on. He mounted quickly then set off in pursuit. There was no chance of catching Griggs on the pinto in a straight chase, but he had an idea of the geography of the trail. He headed up into the rocky land that bounded the Curly P. He knew that the trail doubled back on itself a couple of times and the burro was ideally suited to going over the top.

It was a rough ride, but ten minutes later he spied Griggs on a trail below him. He sped down, the burro valiantly trying to maintain its balance. And then he was almost on top of him.

'Griggs!' he cried, as he launched himself from the saddle into mid-air.

The outlaw turned and tried to sway out of the way, but Jake caught him and together they tumbled heavily on to the trail. They came up with flailing fists, trading blow for blow. But sheer determination on Jake's part won through. With a salvo of body-punishing blows he reduced the Marauder to his knees, then with a final chop to the back of the neck he sent him sprawling in the dirt.

When he turned him over with his toe he found that the outlaw had one last insolent grin.

Jake drew his weapon and ratcheted back the hammer.

'That's right, put me out of my misery, eh, Scudder?'

Jake pointed the gun between Grigg's eyes then slowly shook his head. Instead, he raised it above his head and fired twice in the air. 'I reckon not. You didn't pull the trigger on me, so I'm returning the favour. I'm just letting the posse know where we are. I reckon there'll be a rope waiting for you.'

12

The trial of Frank Griggs took place a week later, when a circuit judge could be brought in from the neighbouring territory and a new sheriff had been appointed. Jubal Jones, the liveryman, had been a popular choice and the whole town backed him when he applied to the judge to have all charges against Jake Scudder dropped.

Frank Griggs was found guilty of several crimes, not least the murder of Deputy Luke Curren and his partner in crime, Ruby-May Prescott. He was sentenced to be hanged and ironically was taken to the state penitentiary in the repaired caboose, hauled by the retrieved and restored Prairie Rose, which he and his Marauders had caused to crash.

The extent of Ruby-May Prescott and Sheriff Dan Foster's duplicity came as a great shock to the towns-people of Coopersville, as their whole plan came to light. They had orchestrated the murder of the town's banker Wilber Sommerton, then of Hank Lassiter; arranged the locomotive crash to rob the bank's money and the kidnapping of Beth Lassiter, with the intention of murdering her too.

The surviving Marauders had testified against Griggs and received shorter sentences than they probably deserved.

'And between them Ruby-May and Sheriff Foster planned to double-cross Griggs as soon as they could,' mused Baxter Walsh, as he sat in the plush dining-room of his friend, Zach Harding's ranch house at the Lazy H.

Soong Zedong, the old Chinese cook, had conjured up a meal to be savoured, and which was indeed enjoyed by Beth Lassiter, her fiancé Todd Brodie, still nursing a shoulder wound, Zach Harding and Jake Scudder.

'Yeah, they were playing for high stakes,' Zach agreed. 'They wanted

Coopersville to become the biggest town in the territory and they worried that Baxter here might buy Hank Lassiter's spread and cut through to the south, then the town might just die.'

'And that was why they fell in with Frank Griggs and his Marauders?' asked Beth.

'I reckon they created the Marauders and gave them all their opportunities; fed them information,' said Jake. 'And when they saw me coming — well, I was just an expendable drifter they had no compunction about using.'

He nodded, then stood up slowly. 'Folks, I'm going to leave you now. It's been a pleasure knowing you all.'

Todd grasped his hand with his free one. 'You're going to be missed, you know.' And Beth reached up and kissed his cheek.

'Are you sure you won't stay and have a hand of cards, or something?' Zach Harding asked. He touched his ear, where a neat little semi-circular notch had been gouged out by Baxter

Walsh's bullet. 'We could do with another poker player here, you know. Although Baxter here is probably the best player I've ever seen. I really thought he couldn't care less whether Dan Foster shot me or not.'

Walsh grinned. 'I just called his bluff, that's all. You would have done the same, Zach.'

'So won't you take a chance and stick around, Jake,' Walsh added. 'I'm sure we can find something round here to make you stay.'

'To tell you all the truth,' Jake said, 'I've just about taken all the chances I feel like taking for the rest of my life.'

And as they all stood on the veranda and watched the tall man ride off, none of them believed that to be true.

THE END

We do hope that you have enjoyed reading this large print book.

Did you know that all of our titles are available for purchase?

We publish a wide range of high quality large print books including:
Romances, Mysteries, Classics
General Fiction
Non Fiction and Westerns

Special interest titles available in large print are:
The Little Oxford Dictionary
Music Book, Song Book
Hymn Book, Service Book

Also available from us courtesy of Oxford University Press:
Young Readers' Dictionary
(large print edition)
Young Readers' Thesaurus
(large print edition)

For further information or a free brochure, please contact us at:
Ulverscroft Large Print Books Ltd.,
The Green, Bradgate Road, Anstey,
Leicester, LE7 7FU, England.
Tel: (00 44) **0116 236 4325**
Fax: (00 44) **0116 234 0205**

Other titles in the
Linford Western Library:

THE LAST WATER-HOLE

Jack Sheriff

When ex-outlaw Bobbie Lee sees a rider approaching Beattie's Halt he expects trouble. Soon, his innocent son is gunned down in the saloon where Van Gelderen, the killer, is later joined by three more strangers. But who are they? When a second young man dies, the strangers leave town. But murder cannot go unpunished . . . Bobbie Lee, Will Blunt and his daughter, Cassie, trail the killers. In the scorching heat of the desert, old feuds will be settled in a six-gun blaze.

A MAN CALLED SAVAGE

Sydney J. Bounds

In New York, an agent hired by the head of the Pinkerton agency would gain the respect of any law-breaker. But is Allan Pinkerton mistaken with this baby-faced killer named Savage? His task: to break up two gangs terrorizing the south-west. Armed with a shotgun — and his concealed knife — he must infiltrate and destroy both gangs, a seemingly impossible mission. Can he justify Pinkerton's faith, or will he die of lead poisoning?

SIX-GUN PRODIGAL

Ken Brompton

Lew Clennan returned to Tinkettle Basin with a price on his head, a six-gun at his hip and a grudge. His bushwhacked father and brothers lay in their graves in the basin, where the vicious code of the grass-war now held sway. Clennan rode a jump ahead of the bounty hunters to buck landgrabber Eli Brix, his gunhawks and crooked hangers-on. Soon the whole basin knew that the six-gun prodigal was back on the scene in pursuit of vengeance.

STAGE RAIDER

Luther Chance

The stage out of Harper's Town bound for Rainwater was late leaving — a bad omen for driver Charlie Deakin. The passenger list caused him further anxiety, including as it did the troublesome banker Willard Pierce and his provocative wife Madelaine; the salacious storekeeper, Lemuel Buthnott; the stranger, Holden; and gunslinger Mr Jones. Then there was the desert route, which Charlie hated, and the prospect of unwelcome riders approaching fast in a cloud of dust. Bad omens could sometimes only get darker . . .

SILVER CREEK TRAIL

David Bingley

In Silver Creek, it seemed that Dan Lawrence had been involved with two successive shooting deaths. So there was little wonder when he panicked and took off for parts unknown. His employer, Hector Morissey, had guaranteed Dan's appearance in court with $10,000, which he now stood to lose. Morissey's detective brother, Ed, went after Dan, risking his life against the bullets of Dan's outlaw associates. But Dan's final determination to do what was right made it all worthwhile.

DEAD MAN'S HAND

John Dyson

Sixty thousand dollars had been stolen from the Central Pacific, the second biggest train robbery in the US. Less than half had been recovered, and the authorities wanted to know why. Texas Ranger Clint Anderson rode south of the border, in search of the lost loot, not suspecting the trouble ahead. Pitted against corrupt *rurales*, bloodthirsty *bandidos* and backstabbers from his own brigade, whom can he trust? And as his battle reaches an explosive climax, will he lose all?